I0642213

Philip Bourke Marston

Song-tide

And other Poems

Philip Bourke Marston

Song-tide
And other Poems

ISBN/EAN: 9783744765718

Printed in Europe, USA, Canada, Australia, Japan

Cover: Foto ©Andreas Hilbeck / pixelio.de

More available books at **www.hansebooks.com**

SONG-TIDE,

AND OTHER POEMS.

SONG-TIDE,

AND OTHER POEMS.

BY

PHILIP BOURKE MARSTON.

BOSTON :

ROBERTS BROTHERS.

MDCCCLXXI.

TO, THE MEMORY OF

ONE WHOSE LOVE WAS THE CHIEF JOY OF MY LIFE,

AND WHOSE LOSS

IS ITS INCONSOLABLE AFFLICTION,

THIS, MY FIRST BOOK,

IS DEDICATED.

CONTENTS.

SONNETS : SONG-TIDE.

CONTENTS.

CONTENTS. ix

SONNETS.

SONG-TIDE.

SONG-TIDE.

PRELUDE.

HEAR'ST thou upon the shore line of thy life,
  The beating of this song-tide led by thee,
  As by the winds, and moon, is led the sea?
The clashing waves conflicting meet in strife,
  Bitter with tears of hopeless love they roll,
  And fall, and thunder, between soul and soul.
Strange things are borne upon their foaming heights,
Through wild, gray windy days, and shrieking nights;
O'er rocks and hidden shoals, round beacon lights,
  Their foam is blown, till on thy shores at length
  They burst, in all the trouble of their strength.

Sad things, O love ! upon thy shore they cast—
    Waifs from the wreck of that fair dream of joy
    With which the winds of Fortune love to toy,
Whereto the waves seem kind, until at last
    The tempest burst upon it, in its might;
    But through the utter darkness of the night,
The happy haven lights, shone calm and clear
Of that loved land so far, and yet so near.
No voice was left to call, no hand to steer,
    It fell before the tempest blind and strong,
    To float a wreck upon this tide of song.

This bitter tide, by winds of passion moved;
    This stormy tide, that wraps and bears its dead;
    This tide, from all strong springs of sorrow fed,
Flowing between my soul and thine beloved;
    This tide, that knows no moon by night, by day
    No burning sun to flame upon its way;
This passionate, strong tide, whose waste waves roll,
And call from one soul to another soul;
This tide that knows the tempest, and the shoal,
    The utter darkness, and at best such light
    As comes between the day-fall and the night.

SONG-TIDE.

Dead hopes, spoiled dreams, sad memories that ache,
    Desires whose hopes were vain, poor, sterile prayers ;
    Such things as these to thee this tide upbears.
Hear where the song waves roar, and where they break,
    Let the sharp sound of woe assail thine ears,
    Even as his who on some midnight hears
Upon a close, and yet night-hidden strand,
The roused sea calling to the silent land,
The strong sea stricken of the storm wind's hand ;
    And as he listens, feels himself the pain
    Of shipwrecked men, who battle with the main.

Hear it again, in some less stormy mood,
    As one who, waking from a dreamless sleep,
    Hears the complaining of a moonless deep,
And feels its vast and endless solitude,
    With sense of wants untold, his heart oppress ;
    With terrible strong yearnings to express
All life's untold, unmeasurable woe,
To look past unrevealing stars, and know
Whereto at length, men's prayers and yearnings go.
    Once, only once, with purged, and holy eyes,
    To see, and know, the promised Paradise.

O love ! my land whereto I may not come,
   Is not my spirit to thy spirit set?
   Hear once, O love ! then, if you can, forget,
For when death makes my lips, and your lips, dumb,—
   When you have done with pity, I with grief,
   When no hope comes to comfort or deceive,
This tide shall flow unchanged upon its way,
And men who catch its beat will surely say,
When comes such love to us in this our day ?
   What must have been the soul that thus could move
   One human spirit to such mighty love ?

Small music in its voice this song-tide has,
   Not strength enough, perchance, to stir one heart ;
   No sun, no moon, to it their light impart,
No happy stars above it shining pass ;
   The summer wots not of it, and no spring,
   With winds that sigh, too full of peace to sing,
Can hope to ease it from the tempest's blast ;
Between the future and the distant past,
It roars and rolls, its waves fall thick and fast,
   Whirled madly by wild winds, and only warm
   With pulse and passion of the viewless storm.

SONG-TIDE.

SONNET I.

A GREETING.

RISE up, my song! stretch forth thy wings and fly
   With no delaying, over shore, and deep!
   Be with my lady when she wakes from sleep;
Touch her with kisses softly on each eye;
And say, before she puts her dreams quite by—
   Within the palaces of slumber keep
   One little niche wherein sometimes to weep,
For one who vainly toils till he shall die.
   Yet say again, a sweeter thing than this;
   His life is wasted by his love for thee.
Then, looking o'er the fields of memory,
   She'll find perchance, o'ergrown with grief and bliss,
Some flower of recollection, pale and fair,
That she, through pity, for a day may wear.

SONNET II.

THE LAST BETROTHED.

In places that have known my lady's grace,
  Seeing how all my soul and life lay there,
  I sat; when, lo, so sitting, I was 'ware
Of breath that fell in sighs upon my face,
While like a harp, wherethrough the night wind plays
  A sorrowful, delicious, nameless air,
  A voice wherein I felt my soul had share
Made music in the consecrated place.
Then, lifting up my eyes, I looked, and lo!
  A fair sad woman sitting all alone
  Where Love brief while ago had made his throne :
Against her pale still breast I leant my brow,
Thy name, I said, is Grief; take then my vow
  That I and thou henceforward be as one.

SONNET III.

WEDDED GRIEF.

AND now we walk together, she and I;
  She sits with me unseen where men are gay,
  And all the pleasures of the sense have sway;
She walks with me beneath the moonlit sky
And murmurs ever of the days gone by;
  She follows still in dreams upon my way,
  She sits beside me in the fading day,
And thrills the twilight silence with a sigh;
So on we journey till we gain the strand
Whose sea conjectures of no further land;
  There, where the past is fading from my view,
To this my sorrow I will reach my hand
And say—O thou who wert alone found true,
Forgive if now I must forget thee too.

SONNET IV.

UNUTTERED THOUGHTS.

HAVE I not bared my soul, O love, to thee,
　　And told thee of the things that sorrow said,
　　When joy went out from life and hope was dead?
I would that this life's song of mine should be
　　A song to cleave unto thy memory.
I have not made my soul a peaceful bed,
The worms of sin upon its dust are fed,
　　And hell makes mirth at its mortality.
　　I have not spared to cloud thy heart with dole ;
But in my breast strange secret thoughts there lie
Whereof no song of mine shall testify.
　　Then by the song and silence of my soul,
The thoughts that live and pass without a cry,
　　Know thou of this, my love, the very whole.

.

SONNET V.

A LAKE.

OH, soul serene ! like some fair, placid lake,
   That flows on silently 'neath day and night,
   What if my spirit, dazed with heat and light,
Dropped, drowned in thee ; shall a leaf falling make
Thy surface troubled, or a light wind shake
   Thy tranquil depths that ever flow aright?
   Oh, cold and lovely lake ! what tempest's might
Shall ever thy smooth currents part or break ?
   Thy great calm beauty can reflect the sun ;
The stars are mirrored in thee, and the moon
   Beholds her image in thy waveless flow,
So cold, and yet so fair to look upon ;
So cold that, even in love's hottest noon,
   Thy depths untroubled are more cold than snow.

SONNET VI.

ANTICIPATION.

How shall it profit me to love thee so?
  What shall I gain for all my love, save tears,
  To make more grievous still my grievous years?
Or shall the bliss of half a year ago,
Comfort my spirit when it comes to know
  How all breath-taking hopes, all joyous fears,
  Are buried deep where no man sees or hears;
While on their grave no gladdening blossoms blow?
Before this fatal love o'erwhelm me quite,
  Be something different, sweet, to what thou art.
Alter, or hide thy beauty from my sight,
  Reverse thy nature, or release my heart;
Let not grief gather strength by much delay;
O love, what thou hast made canst thou not slay?

SONNET VII.

TOO NEAR.

So close we are, and yet so far apart,
  So close, I feel your breath upon my cheek ;
  So far, that all this love of mine is weak
To touch in any way your distant heart ;
So close, that, when I hear your voice, I start
  To see my whole life standing bare and bleak ;
  So far, that though for years and years I seek,
I shall not find thee other than thou art ;
  So, while I live, I walk upon the verge
  Of an impassable and changeless sea
Which more than death divides me, love, from thee :
The mournful beating of its leaden surge
Is all the music now that I shall hear ;
O love, thou art too far, and yet too near.

SONNET VIII.

THE LAST LOOK.

My soul, before we altogether quit
  This land wherein we once had hoped to dwell,
  Take one last look, yea, take one brief farewell.
There shine the paths that now her spirit's feet
Shall tread alone, since, soul, it was not meet
  That thou shouldst walk with her's, yet why rebel?
  Such things we know must be, and who shall tell
What might have been, had she to save thought fit.
  Turn round, my soul, thyself unto the sea
That we must cross; ' is not the harvest past,
  The summer ended?   And we are not saved!'
  Strange hands to us across the sea are waved,
  Strange voices rise and call tumultuously,
And hell laughs out for joy, and cries at last!

SONNET IX.

A VAIN WISH.

I WOULD not, could I, make thy life as mine,
  Only I would, if such a thing might be,
  You should not, love, forget me utterly;
Yea, when the sultry stars of summer shine
On dreaming woods, where nightingales repine,
  I would that at such times should come to thee
  Some thought, not quite unmixed with pain, of me,
Some little sorrow for a soul's decline. .
Yea, too, I would that through thy brightest times,
  Like the sweet burden of remembered rhymes,
That gentle sadness should be with thee, dear;
  And when the gates of sleep are on thee shut,
I would not even then, it should be mute,
But murmur, shell-like, at thy spirit's ear.

SONNET X.

LOVE AND FORGETFULNESS.

CAN I not find in sleep some hidden place
 Whereto, upon some midnight, I may bring
 The image of my love ; some dark, deep spring,
Wherein no stars are mirrored, and no rays
Of moonlight fall ; and there a little space
 Look long into her eyes, imagining
 Some strange, and now impossible sweet thing?
Then, turning, put one hand before my face,
And with the other seize her image fair,
 And cast it down into the water deep,
And see my old dreams pass me voiceless by,
 Ended, as is some dead man's dying prayer :
And so returning from the land of sleep,
Rise up, be glad, nor know the reason why?

SONNET XI.

A SUMMER DREAM.

THERE was a man who through long winter days
  Walked, sadly without hope, until the spring
  Came back to make the whole world shine and sing;
And then he found one day a gracious place
Girt round with trees; while over waving ways
  Of deep green grass the gusty winds did bring
  Soft, subtle scents of sweet flowers blossoming,
With sound of wild birds singing face to face.
There he lay down, and dream'd a dream most fair,
  And, as he slept, through all his dream he felt
  The golden beauty of the summer melt.
How long he slept he knew not, till one day
He woke, and, when his long sleep ebbed away,
Rose up and shivered in gray winter air.

SONNET XII.

KNOWN TOO WELL.

Lo ! now, how well I know the thing thou art ;
　Not more the colour of your hair and eyes
　I know than all your various tones and sighs ;
The laugh half-song, half-moan, that comes to part
The low clear voice, and placid as the heart, ·
　Which, being stainless, needeth no disguise,
　Serene and pure as moonlit seas and skies
Wherethrough no thunders roll, no lightnings dart.
　The music of your voice by heart I have ;
　Yea, every tone, and semi-tone, I know ;
The sound of taken breath, divinely sweet,
The touch of fingers, and the fall of feet ;
I know you better than the wind the wave,
　The sun the heavens, or the Alps the snow.

SONNET XIII.

EXPIATION.

O LOVE ! if I have ever in thee wrought
 The slightest grief, or for the smallest space
 Troubled the happy calmness of thy face,
Then may my soul be blasted by the thought :
May it be made my curse, till I am brought,
 Through nights of anguish, and through bitter days,
 To stand at length before God's judgment place,
Where all man's strength comes utterly to nought.
 Then, though on earth I had grown good as Christ,
 Done all fair, righteous things, and sacrificed
Myself for man, God shall no mercy show,
 But damn me utterly ; and should Christ turn
 To plead, His intercession I will spurn ;
And say — Nay, God, 'tis just ; Lord, even so.

SONNET XIV.

BITTER GIFTS.

My captive soul knelt at my lady's feet,
   And said, 'O queen, what are thy gifts to me?'
   All strong, and pale, and mute, it knelt, and she,
Seeing its capture utter and complete,
Sighed just a little and looked down on it,
   And said, 'I would that I could make thee free,
   For, lo! the gifts that I must give to thee
Are bitter gifts indeed, and no way sweet.'
   Then, with a robe the folds whereof were fire,
   She clothed my soul in unfulfilled desire,
And crowned it with a crown of grief, and said,
   'Rise up! go forth, and labour in thy day.'
So crowned with grief, with torture garmented,
   My soul arose and, speechless, went its way.

SONNET XV.

LOVE'S DESPERATION.

SINCE, sweet, you cannot love me, and we twain
   Must live and die apart ; and since I know,
   Though you, through pity, will not own it now,
Sundered, your soul from mine will not retain
The memory of love, as strong as vain ;
   Full soon you will forget to grieve, and so
   Forget for what you wish to grieve ; and lo !
Once gone, you will not think of me again.
Oh, loved, unloving love ! let not this be.
   Rather, O my love, hate me, with the whole
   Deep strength of thine unfathomable soul.
Yea, let thy hate be as my love for thee ;
   Let it a brand upon my soul be set.
   O love, do everything but this,—Forget !

SONNET XVI.

A POEM.

Lo ! even now, on this wild, winter night,
  Yielding to wishes looked far more than said,
  My lady of her spirit-sweetness read,
In tones that ever soothe my soul aright,
Peaceful, and full, and tender as the light
  Down the dim aisles of old cathedrals shed,
  That sweetest poem that her voice first made
Sacred to me, in days when skies were bright.
And, as she read, the vanished June returned,
  And in the 'tranced, gold, sultry, summer weather,
  Once more in our old place we sat together.
Oh, days of joy ! before my heart had learned
  The bitter, bitter truth, whereby at length
  I know love's grief, and passion of its strength.

SONNET XVII.

A MESSAGE TO THE SEA.

Rise up, my song, and plume thy wings for flight !
  For I will have thee fly to a far place,
  Sad with the joy of unreturning days ;
There, evermore 'twixt storm-scarred height and height,
Calm sighs the sea or thunders in its might,
  There goes out down unto the water ways ;
  And, where the winds the fiercest tumults raise,
And waves upon the loudest reefs are white,
  Cry out, O song, to all the sea and say —
  ' Lo ! even he who sent me bade me pray
That thou once more beloved of him wouldst be,
And comfort him again, in the old way :
  That from this new love thou his heart wouldst free
  Wash clean his soul and be again the Sea.'

SONNET XVIII.

LOVE'S STRENGTH.

HAD you but loved me once as I love you,
　　With all my strength of body, heart, and brain,
　　Till nothing, save our love, in life was plain,
I well had borne all else God had to do;
Whether He made you false to me, or drew
　　The soul from forth the body in slow pain,
　　Or set Death like a gulf between us twain,
I still had said (though what God made He slew),
Though she is false to me, or, worse still, dead,
　　Is not my soul yet glorious from her love?
　　If life's cold now, is not the past enough
To keep my spirit warm till life be shed?
　　All strength save Death's upon the past is vain,
　　And in the past do I not live again?

SONNET XIX.

LOVE'S WEAKNESS.

I KNOW if I had loved you, as saints may,
  I had kept mute this love within my breast,
  So high I think you are above the rest,
That what to other women had been play,
Made you just something sorry for one day ;
  One day, not more ; but great love unexpressed,
  Such love as makes death dark and life unblessed,
Is hard to bear, whatever saints may say.
It doubtless had been fair of me and great,
  If I had let you pass and said no word,
    When all my heart was as the heart of one
From whom, as old tales tell, the mystic bird
    Turned slow and sadly, seeing life was done,
As turned your soul from mine, my love, my fate !

SONNET XX.

A DAY'S SECRET.

ABOUT the wild beginning of the Spring,
  There came to me, and all the world, a day
  To prove the Winter wholly gone away.
I said—'O Day, thy lips are sweet to sing,
But surely in thy voice some sweeter thing
  Than thy mere song I find : lo, now I pray,
  Before thou goest, turn to me and say,
Why round thee so my heart keeps wandering ?'
  Then, as a man who having loved and lost,
  Within his dead love's sister's child may see
Something of what on earth he treasured most ;
  So, looking on that day, my memory
Was filled with thoughts of April days wherein
Love's joy, too young for pain, did first begin.

SONNET XXI.

PERSISTENT MUSIC.

Lo! what am I, my heart, that I should dare
   To love her, who will never love again :
   I, standing out here in the wind and rain,
With feet unsandalled, and uncovered hair,.
Singing sad words to a still sadder air,
   Who know not even if my song's refrain —
   ' Of sorrow, sorrow! loved, oh, loved in vain !'—
May reach her where she sits and hath no care.
But I will sing in every man's despite ;
   Yea, too, and love, and sing of love until
My music mixes with her dreams at night ;
   That when Death says to me, ' Lie down, be still !'
She, pausing for my voice, and list'ning long,
May know its silence, sadder than its song.

SONNET XXII.

SIX MONTHS AGO.

Six months ago, and what thing is the same?
  Here in this garden, where the sweet June day
  Sunk into sleep, while starry stillness lay
Like peace on all, last night the winter came
With stormy winds made strong to smite, and maim
    The well-loved trees, whose boughs, now bare and gray,
    Toss helplessly from side to side and pray
Once more to feel the summer's touch of flame ;
Six months ago, when, half afraid, I said,
  ' Can God's heart be relenting? Ere I go
Shall even I stand face to face with bliss?'
    Now all the meaning of that hope I know :
My soul, since consciousness but sorrow is,
I would, O soul, thou wert asleep, or dead.

SONNET XXIII.

LOVE'S CONQUEROR.

BEHOLD, O Love ! thy conquest is complete ;
   Through every sense thy subtle forces stole,
   Until they won possession of the soul,
Where all is sad and branded by defeat.
Lo ! Peace lies slain, and Hope, with weary feet,
   Returns to me, not having gained the goal.
   Here, all the spring is bloomless, and the whole
Deep music of the sea no longer sweet ;
But only, love, be glad a little space,
   For one, far mightier than thou, shall come
   Who makes the piteous mouths of Sorrow dumb :
Lo ! he shall cast thee down from thy high place ;
No warder when He comes may keep the gate ;
Till then, rejoice : for me, behold I wait.

SONNET XXIV.

THE WIND'S MESSAGE.

I SAID : 'What wouldst thou with my soul to-night,
  Oh ! wild March wind that wailest round the land?
  Tell'st thou of some new grief even now at hand?
Or dost thou in thy swift, and sounding flight,
But chant a requiem for a past delight?
  Like moan of billows on a distant strand,
  Thy message which I fain would understand,
Comes down to me from Heaven's starless height.'
Then sadder wailed the wind, and sadder yet,
  And swept with a great sudden rush of dole
  Across me, till I cried, ' My lady's soul
Is stirred by Pity, and its currents set
To me-ward, and to me she bids thee say—
" Those prayed in vain, grieve more than those who pray." '

SONNET XXV.

BRIEF REST.

O Love ! O lord of all delight, and woe !
  For all who hear, thy voice is still the same ;
  Thy hands cast down the body of wretched shame :
Still to thy chosen children thou dost show
The marvellous, sacred images that glow
  Within thy inmost shrine where one deep flame,
  Intense and clear, of colour without name,
Lights still the carven altars where they bow.
  Brief rest is all I ask, O Love, of thee ;
  A space wherein to look contentedly
Upon the beauty of my lady's face,
And mouth whereof the voice is its best praise ;
  To feel the joy, and not the bitterness,
  Of all her deep and silent loveliness.

SONNET XXVI.

AT DAWN.

HERE, at this day's dawn, desolate and gray,
   Whose light divides the wan and watery skies,
   Seeing with troubled soul and sleepless eyes,
I think upon my love so far away ;
Sees she, as I, the dawning of this day,
   Around whose birth the wind presaging, sighs?
   Or roams her soul the twilight land that lies
'Twixt life and death, wherein all ghosts have sway,
   Wherein the pallid lips of days long dead
Unclose and murmur as they hover round
The souls that thread Sleep's mysteries without sound ?
   Lo ! even now, some day remembered,
May to her heart be saying all I fain
Would say myself, or have her hear again.

SONNET XXVII.

DIVINE PITY.

I WONDER when you've gained the happy place,
 And walked above the marvel of the skies,
 And seen the brows of God, and large sweet eyes
Of Christ look lovingly upon your face,
 And all dear friends of unforgotten days ;
Will you some time in that fair Paradise,
While all its peace and light around you lies,
 To greet your lover lost your dear eyes raise?
And when at length this thing you come to know,
 How he, forbid to pass, the heavenly bourne,
 Through undreamed distance roves with shades forlorn,
Will you be sorry, and, with eyes bent low,
 Wander apart the sudden wound to hide,
 And, meeting Mary, turn your face aside?

SONNET XXVIII.

TWILIGHT VIGIL.

HERE in the stillness of this fading day,
  Moveless, with lips apart and folded eyes,
  Lovely in dreamless calm my lady lies ;
And, as one, who by some long weary way,
Gaining the land he longed for, will delay
  His sleep at night, because in heart he tries
  To walk once more 'neath bleak and unloved skies,
And lose this azure in their distant gray,
  That he may start with rapturous surprise,
To find his bliss not false ; so even now
  From looking on her loveliness I turn
To fancy that the seas between us flow.
  Oh, shame, my heart, for dost thou not discern
That gulfs impassable between us rise ?

SONNET XXIX.

REMEMBERED WORDS.

Lo ! 'mid the fall and ruin of my days,
  One thing is sweet for my remembering,
  Those words which all my strength of love did wring
From out my.lady's soul when, face to face,
We stood together for a little space ;
  She felt my spirit to her spirit cling,
  From every look she saw love break, and spring,
And how my soul was shaken to its base ;
Then from my passion, turning half away,
Her heart conceived, and her lips found to say,
  The words whereby my soul is comforted ;
  Whereby my unbelieving heart was led
At length to know her soul believed the love
That had no way whereby its strength to prove.

SONNET XXX.

DE PROFUNDIS.

OUT of the depths, love, have I called to thee;
   Love, hear my voice, consider well, O love,
   The voice of my complaint.   If prayers could move
Thy heart, O love! then wouldst thou pity me.
Look thou deep down into my soul and see
   The way in which I love thee; test, and prove
   The spirit's passion and the strength thereof.
O my beloved! through change of years to be,
   My life henceforth for thee anew begins.
If I in heaven should thy rapture mar,
I 'gainst myself the gates of peace would bar,
   But shouldst thou have a whim to save my soul,
   Then will I strive indeed to reach the goal,
   And thou shouldst me redeem from all my sins.

SONNET XXXI.

LOVE'S YEARNINGS.

I WOULD I could believe the words men say,
  And think, despite of all, there ruled above,
  Some sure strong God compassionate enough
To hear and pity spirits when they pray;
That so from day to night, from night to day,
  In passionate strong praying I might prove
  The height, breadth, depth, and length of all my love.
So when soft dreams upon thy spirit lay,
  I, sleepless, had devised sweet things for thee,
Poured forth my soul in prayer, nor let God rest,
  Till he had heard my prayers, and answered all.
  Prayers have I, but no God at need to call.
  Then, in the absence of all Deity,
Still show me, love, how I may serve thee best.

SONNET XXXII.

VAIN LOVE.

I WOULD the wide waste waters of the deep
   Had met above me ere my eyes had seen
   The face of her who is my spirit's queen,
Or would that Death had met with me in sleep,
And taken me to where none laugh or weep,
   Ere I had felt her hands on my hands lean :
   From out the fields of life shall I not glean
One year of joy, while others harvests reap?
   I would some snake about my life had wound,
Ere in the calm, ineffable and sweet,
Of that strange voice my soul had lain a space,
   Faint, trembling in a Paradise of sound,
How shall I bear once more her look to meet
And feel we walk apart in separate ways?

SONNET XXXIII.

ASSOCIATIONS.

SWEET is the voice that sings, and sweet the air,
  But only sweet to me, because they bring
  Back perfectly to my remembering
A tune as sad, and passionate as pray'r,—
A tune I heard when life and love were fair.
  When all the strong, sweet perfumes of the spring
  Did so about my lady's presence cling,
They seemed her very loveliness to share.
So, when I hear this tune, that other strain
Revives within me, and I see again
My lady's face ; yea, then I do rejoice ;
Recalling half-lost beauties of her voice ;
·A little then the present off I cast,
And walk 'mid lovely ruins of the past.

SONNET XXXIV.

BEFORE SEVERING.

THERE, let me gaze upon you ere I go,
  The supple body and the placid face
  Half known before we met, through old sweet lays,
Or wondered on, with ecstasy, and woe,
In some great picture such as dead years show;
  But seen, found fairer, in all gracious ways,
  Than these which lack the special, unnamed grace,
Which makes your face the fairest man may know.
  Speak once again, that I may hear your voice,
And madden on the beauty of each tone.
  O love! be sorry for these poor dead joys!
Be sorry, O my sweet, for fair dreams flown.
  You had a little, what in me was best,
  Now let all vile things fatten on the rest.

SONNET XXXV.

RETROSPECT.

OH ! strange to me, and terrible it seems
  To think that, ere I met you, you and I
  Lived both beneath the same all-covering sky,
Had the same childhood's hopes and childhood's schemes,
And, later on, our beautiful false dreams :
  The funerals of my dead joys passed me by,
  And things, expected long, at length drew nigh.
The joy that slays and sorrow that redeems
  Were ours before that day whereon we met ;
  And all the weary way that God had set
Between us was past over, and my soul
Knew in your fatal loveliness its goal.
  'Twas mine to love, 'twas yours, sweet, to forget ;
For you the haven, and for me the shoal.

SONNET XXXVI.

BODY AND SOUL.

ALL know the beauty of my lady's face,
   The peace and passion of her deep grey eyes,
   Her hair wherein gold warmth of sunlight lies,
Her mouth that makes as mockery all praise,
And languorous low voice that hath such ways
   Of unimagined music that the soul
   Stands poised and trembling ; breathless till the whole
Ends in an unhoped symphony of sighs :
But who as I my lady's soul shall know—
   The deep tides of her nature that bear on,
   Till all the line of common life seems gone,
To hearts that weary of their boundaries grow,
Then must I turn, O love, from thee to go
   Through ways, to places, of thy soul unknown?

SONNET XXXVII.

DISTANT LIGHT.

OH, when, love, do I think upon thee most?
　When life looks blackest, and when hope seems dead,
　When darkness over all the past is shed,
When, as men hear upon some darkened coast,
The distant tumult of the ocean's host,
　I hear the future sound in places dread
　Through which full soon my spirit must be led.
Then does my soul, through sorrow well-nigh lost,
　Look up to thy soul shining from afar,
　As men at sea look up to some fair star
Whose saving light may point the path to home.
　O love! bear with me for a little space,
　Bear with the roar and tumult of my days,
Till I am past the reach of wind and foam.

SONNET XXXVIII.

WHY DO I LOVE?

WHAT is the thing for which I love thee best?
  It taxes me to say ; but this I know,
  Thy tender regal beauty moves me so
That my heart beats and leaps within my breast,
As might the sea 'twixt narrow shores compressed.
  Haply for this, or smiles that come and go
  About thy mouth, or music sweet and low
Of thy clear voice, wherein is perfect rest,
  Or for high intellect, that as a light
  Lights up thy heart that straight illumes thy face,
Or for thy soul's deep tenderness that flows
  Through every tone, and lingers in thy gaze—
For these known things I love with all my might,
And for the things beyond which no man knows.

SONNET XXXIX.

BEFORE MEETING.

So we shall meet within a little space,
   And on the face wherein no love has birth
   Where nought is clear save beauty and the dearth
Of passions good or ill, I long shall gaze.
We shall not speak at all of vanished days,
   Of years that might have been, and made the earth
   All fair to me ; but words of little worth
Shall pass between us, standing face to face.
  Too well I know the voice that I shall hear,
   When her lips, parting, let out sound more sweet
Than ever fell before on mortal ear.
   Oh, heart of mine, be strong until we meet,
Fill well thy *rôle* before her, O my heart,
Till death shall end the playing of thy part.

SONNET XL.

WASTED STRENGTH.

AND has my love then no more use than this,
   To waste its strength in waves of sterile song
   Upon life's shore while heart and hand are strong
To dare for love's sake every ill that is?
O God! the dying patriot's final bliss,
   Who, though he see his land not free from wrong,
   Knows as he stands above the shrieking throng,
He serves her dying, without crown or kiss,
   The Pagans' joy when for their gods they die
   As Christians for their Christ; I, only I,
Must worship what I may not serve at all.
   Oh, thou, my land, my Christ, my God, my love!
   Find some sure way whereby love's strength to prove,
Ere love and life in one vast ruin fall.

SONNET XLI.

LOVE'S SELFISHNESS.

AND have I no more share in thee, O sweet,
  Than any of the many men who gaze
  Well pleased upon the beauty of the face,
Whose eyes are glad, indeed, your eyes to meet?
I, who have laid my soul beneath your feet,
  I, who upon the ruin of my days
  To thee an everlasting shrine will raise,
That men in coming years with song shall greet;
  I, even I, whose pride it is to bear
  The cross which thou hast laid upon me, love,
  Who give thee bitter songs, as men give prayer
To high and unknown gods, whom no prayers move;
I, who must long for thee through my life's night,
More than the blind man ever longed for light.

SONNET XLII.

LOVE'S MAGNETISM.

O LOVE! though far apart our bodies be,
   I think my soul must somehow touch your heart,
   And make you, in the dusk of slumber start,
To feel my strong love beat and surge round thee,
Oh, one sweet island of my soul's waste sea.
   Serene and fair, and passionless thou art,
   Why should my sorrow of thy life make part,
Or shade the face burnt in my memory?
I think, too, as I pace the tawny sand,
If you were on the opposite fair strand,
And my heart should with love to your heart yearn,
I do believe you could not choose but turn
And look across the sea, my way, until
Not knowing why, my soul should burn and thrill.

SONNET XLIII.

LOVE'S SHRINES.

ALL places that have known my love at all
   Have grown as sympathetic friends to me,
   And each for song has some dear memory,
Some perfume of her presence clings to all ;
How then, to me, O love, shall it befall,
   When I no longer in my life shall see
   The places that through love have grown to be
Of buried dreams the mute memorial ?
   Then surely shall I seem as one who stands
   Exiled from home in unfamiliar lands,
And strains across the weary sea and long
   His desolate sad eyes, and wrings his hands,
While round him press an undiscerning throng
Of strange men talking in an alien tongue.

SONNET XLIV.

SEVERED FOR EVER.

O LOVE, when the great gulfs between us are,
  When all is said that you or I can say,
  When you have made your choice and gone your way,
While in strange lands, unlit by any star,
But full of storm and flame and all the jar
  Of shrill strained music such as fiends may play,
  When on some soul, long waited for as prey,
Their hands the gates of hell in thunder bar,
  I walk, and heap new nights and barren days
Upon my weary soul to keep your face
  From rising up to look at me, and press
Upon me with its old sweet influence,
  Then you may know, across a dead soul's grave,
  How love is strong to slay as well as save.

SONNET XLV.

LOVE PAST UTTERANCE.

I AM a painter, and I love you so
   I cannot paint your face for very love ;
   My heart is like a sea the tempests move
Wherein no ship a certain path may know ;
I can but gaze upon you till you grow
   Lovely and distant as the skies above :
   How then to man shall I my worship prove,
And unto coming worlds your beauty show ?
   I am a poet, and my love is such
      I cannot tell the marvel of your voice,
Or show the laugh that thrills me like a kiss ;
   The very recollection of your touch
      O'ercomes me like a sudden tide of joys,
And my heart gasps for breath 'twixt waves of bliss.

SONNET XLVI.

UNSOLVED.

MAIMED from my birth and nowise fair to see,
 The soul in me a-flame was keen and strong
 To shape my sorrows into burning song;
Such was I when she first discovered me.
O face, O voice, O one sweet memory!
 Her touch I thought a trifle just too long
 For mere indifference, but I did her wrong
To think upon a thing that could not be.
I said—'tis only pity makes her kind,
 I will not vex her by a useless pain;
 And so I left the sunlight of her face.
Now I am old, not only maimed, but blind,
 I cannot guess if love did wax or wane,
And God alone her spirit's veil shall raise.

SONNET XLVII.

HOPELESS LOVE.

SHE came to me as comes some time in sleep
  A mystic midnight vision strange and fair,
  The beauty of her presence tranced the air;
And, as she came, I felt my soul up-leap
To see her face and for pure passion weep;
  She paused a moment and swept back her hair,
  And looked upon my face, as seeking there
  Some little sign in after years to keep;
Then, mad with love and strong with love's despair,
  With open arms her path to bar I strove:
    But, said she—I must pass; so I gave way,
But felt first then the barrenness of prayer,
  The fearful bitterness of hopeless love:
    My God, which thing is worse, to love or pray?

SONNETS XLVIII., XLIX., L.

SONNETS TO A VOICE.

ˑI.

ROSSINI, and Beethoven, and Mozart,
 And all the other men of mighty name
 Together joined their previous work to shame ;
The subtlest mystery of their god-like art
To that most magic voice they did impart.
 Oh, from what kingdom of rare music came
 A voice on which alone might rest such fame
As never yet made glad one mortal's heart ?
 A star of sound set far above the din
  And dust of life, a shade wherein to lie
Faint with the sudden ecstasy of bliss,
 A voice to drown remembrance of sin,
  A voice to hear and for the hearing die,
As Antony for Cleopatra's kiss !

II.

A CLEAR voice made to comfort and incite,
  Lovely and peaceful as a moonlit deep,
  A voice to make the eyes of strong men weep
With sudden overflow of great delight;
A voice to dream of in the calm of night,
  A voice—the song of fields that no men reap,
  A treasure wrung by God himself from sleep !
A voice no song may follow in its flight,
  A queenly rose of sound with tune for scent,
A pause of shadow in a day of heat,
  A voice to make God weak as any man,
  And at its pleadings take away the ban
'Neath which so long our spirits have been bent,
  A voice to make death tender and life sweet !

III.

THERE is no sound at all in heaven now ;
  God and His angels bow from their high place
To hear the smallest word which that voice says,
  And they do well indeed to listen so ;
  For they can hear it though its tones are low,
They must have learnt by heart its gracious ways,
  Its fluctuant languor, and low laughter's grace —
Such tune as man again shall never know.
  O winds! O birds ! O rushing streams and seas !
And all things that make music for a space,
  Dry up, grow mute ; for one who hears that voice
  Can no more in your lesser sounds rejoice.
O voice of rest, O amplitude of peace,
  Sound deified—a bliss that beggars praise !

SONNET LI.

A VISION OF DAYS.

THE days whereof my heart is still so fain
    Passed by my soul in strange and sad procession,
    And one said—Lo, I held thy love's confession ;
And one—my hands were filled with golden gain
Of thy love's sweetnesses now turned to pain ;
    And one —I heard thy soul's last sad concession ;
    And one--for thee my voice made intercession ;
And one—I wept above thy sweet hopes slain.
Then followed, in a long and mournful band,
    Days wreathed with cloud and garmented with grey,
    And all made moan upon their weary way;
But one day walked apart ; and, in her hand,
Before her face, she held a sorcerer's wand—
    And what she said I heard, but may not say.

SONNET LII.

PARTING WORDS.

Good-bye, O love, once more I hold your hand :
  Good-bye, for now the wind blows loud and long ;
  The ship is ready, and the waves are strong
To bear me far away from this thy strand :
I know the sea that I shall cross, and land
  Whereto I journey, and the forms that throng
  Its palaces and shrines ; I know the song
That they alone can sing and understand.
  But promise me, O love, before I go
  That sometimes, when the sun and wind are low,
You, walking in the old familiar ways
Thronged with grey phantoms of the buried days,
  Will, looking seaward, say I wonder now
  How fares it with him in the distant place ?

SONNET LIII.

PRESENTIMENT.

WHEN, after parting long and sore, we twain
  Met and stood soul to soul as face to face,
  While yet her hand in mine was, and her gaze
Made the blood burn and leap through every vein—
When thus, 'twixt risen joy and fallen pain,
  We stood with love in his own time and place,
  My soul had foresight of the coming days
When, parted, we should never meet again.
  O days expected long, and are ye here?
  Come ye with clouded brows and eyes austere,
Or with blithe faces making glad the sight,
  I know your song for curse, your laugh for jeer:
Which, then, is worse—your mockery of light,
Or the dumb darkness of the hopeless night?

SONNET LIV.

LOVE AND HOPE.

A VOICE within me whispered—hope is sped :
　He will not stir again so still he lies.
　Alas ! for all his sweet false prophecies,
Love sits and weeps above his silent bed ;
　His life is ended as a tune outplayed.
But while the voice was speaking in this wise,
My lady came and said,—' Forbear thy sighs,
　For sleep, not death, upon this hope is laid.'
Thereat hope rose, and smiled a little space ;
　But after this came love to me, and said—
' No sleep but death now on thy hope is shed.'
　Then came my lady, and with steadfast gaze
Looked on me and passed by with bended face,
And so I knew that hope indeed was dead.

SONNET LV.

LOVE'S MUSIC.

LOVE held a harp between his hands, and lo !
  The master hand, upon the harp-strings laid,
  By way of prelude, such a sweet tune played
As made the heart with happy tears o'erflow ;
But sad and wilder did that music grow,
  And, like the wail of woods by storm gusts swayed,
  While yet the awful thunder's wrath is stayed,
And Earth lies faint beneath the coming blow,
  Still wilder waxed that tune ; until at length
The strong strings, strained by sudden stress and sharp,
Of that musician's hand intolerable,
  And jarred by sweep of unrelenting strength,
  Sundered, and all the broken music fell.
Such was Love's music,—lo, the shattered harp !

SONG-TIDE.

SONNET LVI.

SUMMER'S RETURN.

ONCE more I walk 'mid summer days, as one
　　Returning to the place where first he met
　　The face that he till death may not forget;
I know the scent of roses just begun,
And how at evening and at morn the sun
　　Falls on the places that remember yet
　　What feet last year within their bounds were set,
And what sweet things were said, and dreamt, and done :
　　The sultry silence of the summer night
Recalls to me the loved voice far away ;
Oh, surely I shall see some early day,
　　In places that last year with love were bright,
The face of her I love and hear the low,
Sweet, troubled music of the voice I know.

SONNET LVII.

FINIS.

My lady has no heart in her for love :
  Her soul can understand the mountain's peace,
  And the blue quiet of the summer seas,
Or scented warmness of the thick-leaved grove
That hears the low lamenting of one dove ;
  But when the skies grow black and winds increase,
  And rains and sudden lightnings charge the trees,
And seas at length in strife begin to move,
She only joyless stands 'mid flame and noise
  Of storms that rend the night and lift the main ;
Her griefs are pale, and flameless all her joys :
  How should she know, then, love's great bliss and pain ?
  O love, has all my singing been in vain ;
My songs are ended ; hast thou heard no voice?

POEMS.

ON THE DEATH OF ROSSINI.

DEATH, who has called thy brothers, has called thee;
And not alone doth sacred Italy,
That gave thee birth, mourn her set star, but we
Of England's misty clime and sea-washed shore,
And they of sunny France, thy loss deplore.
The sorrow spreads, till mighty Germany
Takes up the wail.   All Europe bows the knee.

Not as one star that in a waste of night
Looks clear, because there is no greater light
To shine upon the world and daze the sight—
Not so wast thou; for round thee on each hand
Were men in whose great company to stand
Meant life with gods; but by thy greater might
Of music wast thou Lord and King by right.

Thy strains go with us to the end of days ;
Thy soul cleft through the heavy-hanging haze,
And, passing forth into the pathless ways
And shoreless tides of sounds, thou there didst find
Soft tunes, more soft than the first breath of wind
Which, at a July dawn, doth gently raise
The leaf that drops again into its place :

Softer than is the first delicious sleep
That, after fever fierce, doth gently steep
The wearied soul in quiet dim and deep,
Sadder in sound than unto saddened eyes
The twilight deepening in pale autumn skies,
And sad as thoughts of those who all night weep
By dying souls their mournful watch to keep.

What fire of fury from these moods did turn
Thy soul, and make thy kindling blood to burn,
And yearn for strife, as does a Chieftain yearn,   .
So that thy music, with impulsive breath
Of glowing life, when life in strife meets death,
Cried with loud lips, whose very joy was stern,
And bade us glory seek and danger spurn—

Hear the keen arrows hissing cleave the air,
And stormy sound of battle everywhere;
But through it comes a sweet-imagined prayer
From those at home, and softens all the jar.
Thus sailors, where the breakers shallower are,
Hear loved ones wail on shore, and know that there
Warm hearts are bowed with grief they scarce can bear.

In what strange dream, upon what alien sea,
Didst thou discover that sweet melody
That is to coming worlds a joy to be?
To us that hear an influence so sweet,
It draws out love, as in the summer, heat
Draws perfume from a faint and flowery lea,
Melting the mist that moves round memory!

O sweet and purest Muse! Thou that dost plead
To speak those thoughts and feelings which, if freed,
Should gladden all who hear, thou hast no need
Of common words, for we who know thy voice
Know well when thou art sad or dost rejoice:
But now bow down thine head, be sad indeed;
Who led thy steps, thy steps no more shall lead.

I see thee stand before me as I write—
Thy lustrous eyes full of soft change and light,
And fair bowed face and lips that are so bright,
Through which he drew the treasures of thy heart,
And to the world their secrets did impart :
Weep now, for he is shorn of all his might,
And knows no more of sorrow or delight.

By thee his thoughts and feelings found their vent ;
And when his soul in thought to battle went,
Or o'er some fair imagined mistress bent,
Thy voice could peal, or murmur like a kiss ;
By thee, through him, we knew a lover's bliss,
Passion and pain and love in one were blent,
His heart o'erflowed and bowed the instrument.

Sometimes he filled thy voice with tender tears,
As of a happy maiden when she nears
The joy she longs for and yet something fears ;
And then with ringing laughter would he fill
Thy strong sweet accents, and, again, make still
The sounds of mirth, and fill our eager ears
With grief that much reveals, yet nothing clears.

His strains come to us now as blows a breeze
Over the vast white weary worlds of seas
From a fair land where dwelt in joy and peace
One whom we loved, but whose bright life has flown ;
Sad must have been the heart whose weary moan
Did not, for some small space of being, cease,
Lulled by the rapture of his harmonies.

And who am I, that with soft words deplore
And weep his death, and know that never more
Shall Italy see on her golden shore
A soul like that which, by Apollo blest,
Has now passed into everlasting rest ?
When shall again such melody out-pour—
Shall that come last that did not come before ?

Surely the Virgin, dwelling pure above,
Felt suddenly her heart surprised with love
As she heard round the gates of heaven move,
Borne up from earth and splendid with her praise
And all the holy triumph of dead days,
His strain of her which surely is enough
To win him heaven and the joys thereof.

Let for one hour his brothers dead arise
To beat with tune the gates of Paradise,
That she the Virgin, holy and most wise,
Remembering all the beauty of that strain,
May plead with Christ and surely not in vain
His immortality, while we with sighs
Envy the new-found rapture of the skies.

Now, Sister Music, living yet, behold
How England, with her strength and gathered gold,
And France, that in her white arms does enfold
The splendour and the pain of great delight,
And Italy, once more made pure and white,
Weep for his death.   Did not the strains that rolled
Through Paris, and the voices manifold,

And subtle fragrance of the funeral rose
Come to him on the languid wind that blows
From life's land to the land of death's repose,
As on one wearied long by sore disease
Who falls asleep, and for a minute sees,
In lulls of consciousness, a face he knows,
And hears a well-known voice that through him flows—

A stream of mingled rapture and of pain ?
So, if he heard, so would he hear that strain
Break in upon his sleep and not in vain,
And know how we all here deplore his end :
A little while on earth our days we spend,
Then pass, with mighty loss and fleeting gain,
To shores of rest across death's waveless main.

O Sister, now to whom wilt thou impart
The many secrets of thy burdened heart ?
What lover fresh for thee from Time shall start
Thy mighty soul to utter, as did he
Who now is gone—ordained to solace thee,
And mourning men, when fate's malignant dart
Struck dead thy lord and lover, great Mozart ?

Two or three still are left to thee ; but they—
Shall they be as the soul that's passed away ?
Let us not weep, and for fresh glories pray :
Though all thy greatest lovers are gone by,
What they have told of thee can never die,
And blest are we because that we can say,
We loved and lived in great Rossini's day.

PAST AND FUTURE.

O Love, once more if we
  Should meet, and once more stand
  Upon the golden strand,
  Between the sea and land,
The green land and the sea,

Should we speak of the past,
  But two brief years gone by,
  When, 'neath the summer sky,
  Was born what shall not die
While life with me shall last !

Shall I recall that day,
  My last of perfect peace,
  When, through the branching trees,
  The gusty summer breeze
Moved singing on its way !

And far off lay the main !
 But we together stood
 Within that well-loved wood ;
 Life looked to me then good,
It looks not so again !

Yes, far off lay the sea,
 And, vaguely and half seen,
 We caught its tender sheen
 Of blue that mixed with green,
As I would mix with thee ;

And hold thee for a space
 Within my arms, O sweet,
 Till heart to heart should beat,
 Until our lips should meet,
As in the dear gone days,

A space wherein to sigh,
 With love and bow my head
 Down to your face, and shed
 My soul for you to tread
Beneath your feet, then die !

But strong is fate, O love,
  Who makes, who mars, who ends,
  Whose strength with weakness blends,
  Who joy with sorrow sends—
Just little joy enough

To mock us, crying—lo,
  What might be, and what is !
  Yea, often falls the kiss,
  The long-desired bliss,
On lips that nothing know.

O love, what did we say ?
  Of course, you cannot tell ;
  And I know yet too well
  Each little word that fell
From your lips on that day !

Yea, I shall see till death
  Your face and deep blue eyes,
  And hear the soft short sighs
  That take, with sweet surprise
Of sound, the rapid breath !

Thy lot is sweet for thee,
  Fair, flowery is thy way;
  With thee 'tis always May,
  My life is cold and grey
As any winter sea !

Perchance you may recall
  That mute warm summer's night,
  When with the moon's clear light
  The sea was calm and bright,
And no wind was at all !

And hardly could the deep
  Get strength to kiss the strand,
  The sea-wet shining sand;
  A spell lay on the land
As of great love and sleep !

Still, love, my sad sight sees,
  As in the days that were,
  Your eyes that would not spare,
  And light of golden hair
As flame blown by a breeze !

Oh, sound of vanished feet,
  Oh, sad remembering .
  In winter of the spring !
  My lips now only sing
Sad songs, and no more sweet !

I shall live on and see
  Fresh people and fresh days,
  But none the reason trace
  Why one name of one place
Is more than tune to me !

But when you hear the name,
  The reason you may find.
  O fair land left behind !
  O sea of summer, blind
With light of summer flame !

Yea, love ! no more may we
  Together walk or stand
  Upon the golden strand,
  Between the sea and land,
The green land and the sea !

SIR LAUNCELOT'S SONG OF GUENEVERE.

She is fresh and she is bright,
Joyous as the morning light;
Tender as a summer night,
Wherein men lose their souls for bliss,
And airs come wafted like a kiss
From crimson lips of Guenevere.
Who so stately, who so fair
As my own love, Guenevere?

When were ever seen such eyes,
Where the love light faints and flies?
Such a crimson paradise
As her sweet mouth rife with love
Murmuring secret joys thereof?
Droop above me, Guenevere!
Who has lips, and eyes, and hair
Like thine own, my Guenevere?

When the sun had left the west,
With head upon her fair white breast,
Oft at night times would I rest,
While, the listening space along,
Poured the music of her song
That told the love of Guenevere.
What in witchery may compare
With the voice of Guenevere?

Who has ever seen such feet,
Round which jewelled sandals meet,
Sweetly indolent or fleet
As love prompts or pleasure stays?
Love shines royal in the face
Of my royal Guenevere.
Love that doth a sceptre bear
Yields it to my Guenevere.

Thrills her touch through pulse and vein,
Flooding each with rapturous pain
That of its excess doth wane ;
Moves she as a laden vine

That doth rise or now decline
As the love-gust sweeps by her;
Who is various, who is fair
As my own love, Guenevere?

La Belle Iseult is fair, we know;
Her mouth a rose, her bosom snow;
Such charms for other men may blow,
Their beauties may, for my will, pass
Like their own semblance in a glass,
If they leave but Guenevere.
Who has brows so fit to wear
Love's crown as my Guenevere?

Morgan le Fay is fair and wise,
With strange words in her lips and eyes,
That read the secrets of the skies;
She's too weird, too grave for me,
Too like a tranced summer sea.
Changeful is my Guenevere;
Whom shall mortal eyes compare
In each change with Guenevere?

BALLAD.

'O MOTHER, the wind wails wearily,
The twilight gathers round the shore
And on the sea;
Oh, loud he cries, love come to me,
And weep no more.
Alas! my love, I am not free,
And my heart is sore.'

'Be still, my daughter, and have no fear,
'Tis but your fancy's idle play,
No sound ye hear
Save winds and breakers roaring near
From the vexed bay;
Be still, my child, my daughter dear,
Wait for the day.'

' O Willie, the night is bleak and bare,
  No moonlight shines upon the main.
            In my gold hair,
  And on my shoulders white and fair,
            I feel the rain.
Willie, my love, where are you, where?
            Do you call in pain?'

' Oh, ask me not too much, my love,
  The starless night is like a pall
            Your truth to prove;
Will you not come through bay and cove,
            Love, when I call—
Thro' waves that white and whirling move,
            Each wave a wall?'

She girt her raiment to her knee,
  She left the barren cliffs behind,
            And to the sea
She set her face right silently.
            ' Love, I am blind,
Oh, guide me as I come to thee,
            Clothed with the wind.

' Blind with the force of beaten foam,
　　Blind with the driven rain and sleet ;
　　　　　O love, I come ;
O love, await me in thy home,
　　　　　Love guide my feet !'
She spake no more ; her lips grew dumb—
　　　　　Red lips and sweet.

AFTER MANY DAYS.

In autumn's silent twilight, sad and sweet,
  O love, no longer mine, alone I stand ;
Listening, I seem to hear dear phantom feet
    Pass by me down the golden wave-worn strand :
      I think of things that were and things that be,
      I hear the soft low ripples of the sea
That to my thoughts responsive music beat.

My heart is very sad to-night and chill,
  But hushed in awe, as his who turns and feels
A mournful rapture through his being thrill,
    When music, sweet and slumb'rous, softly steals
      Down the deep calm of some cathedral nave ;
      Then swells and throbs and breaks as does a wave,
And slowly ebbs, and all again is still.

And is it only five years since, O love,
  That we in this old place stood side by side,
Where in the twilight once again I move ?
  Is this the same shore washed by the same tide ?
    My heart recalls the past a little space,
    The sweet and the irrevocable days;
I knew not then how bitter life might prove.

I loved you then, and shall love till I die ;
  Your way of life is fair, it should be so,
And I am glad, though in dark years gone by
  Hard thoughts of you I had ; but now I know
    A fairer and a softer path was meet
    For treading of your dainty maiden feet :
Your life must blossom 'neath a summer sky.

The twilight, like a sleep, creeps on the day,
  And like dark dreams the night creeps on that sleep ;
If you should come again in the old way
  And look from pensive tender eyes and deep
    Upon me, as you looked in days of old—
    If my hand should again of yours take hold,
How should I feel, and what thing should I say ?

Ah, sweet days flown shall never come again ;
  That happy summer time shall not return
When we two stood beside this peaceful main,
    And saw at eve the rising billows yearn
      With passion to the moon, and heard afar, ·
      Across the waves, and 'neath the first warm star,
From ships at sea some sweet remembered strain.

I can recall the day when first we met,
  And how the burning summer sunlight fell
Across the sea ; nor, love, do I forget
    How, underneath that summer noontide spell,
      We saw afar the white-sailed vessels glide
      As phantom ships upon a waveless tide,
Whose shining calm no breezes come to fret.

And shall I blame you, sweet, because you chose
  A softer path of life than mine could be ?
I keep our secret here, and no man knows
    What passed five years ago 'twixt you and me—
      Two loves begotten at the self-same time,
      When that gold summer tide was in its prime :
One love lives yet, and one died with the rose.

I work and live and take my part in things,
  And so my life goes on from day to day ;
Fruitless the summers, seedless all the springs,
  To him who feels December one with May :
    The night is not more dreary than the sun,
    Not sadder is the twilight, dim and dun,
Than dawn that, still returning, shines and sings.

Fed with wet scent of hills, through growing shades,
  To the white water's edge the wind moans down ;
The lapping tide steals on, while daylight fades,
  And fills the caves with shells and seaweed brown.
    Ah, wild sea-beaten coast, more dear to me
    Than fairest scenes of that fair land could be
Where warm Italian suns steep happy glades !

Farewell, familiar scene, for I ascend
  The jagged path that led me to the shore ;
Farewell to cliff, cave, inlet—each a friend ;
  My parting steps shall visit ye no more :
    Dear are ye all where soft light steals through gloom,
    Here had my joy its birth — here found its tomb —
Here love began, and here one love had end.

OUT OF EDEN.

AGAIN the summer comes, and all is fair;
A sea of tender blue, the sky o'erhead
Stretches its peace; the roses white and red,
    Through the deep silence of the trancéd air,
    In a mute ecstasy of love declare
Their souls in perfume, while their leaves are fed
With dew and moonlight that fall softly shed
    Like slumber on pure eyelids unaware.

O wasted affluence of scent and light!
Each gust of fragrance smites me tauntingly;
Yon placid stars have rankling shafts for me;
    My great despair, by its own fatal might,

Converts to pain the loveliness of night.
Ah, would I could from all this beauty flee,
And, 'neath some grey sky on a cheerless sea,
　　Let drift a life that cannot end aright.

Vain flower of fame from which is gone the scent,
Vain crown no longer glorious in mine eyes,
Vain hopes at which, years back, my joy would rise
　　Like melody within an instrument
　　When skilled hands touch the strings.　All now is spent,
And what is gained?　Lo, I have gained my prize,
And here neglected at my feet it lies;
　　It meant so much: I now ask what it meant.

For thee, lost love, I shall not see again; ·
The pale sad beauty of thy tender face,
Once lamp and light of this now starless place,
　　Comes to me in my dreams, and I am fain
　　To hold thee in my arms, and so retain
Thy phantom form in one long wild embrace;
A flush illumes the features of dead days,
　　But fades before the lights in heaven wane.

I am as one who, in a festive hall
Ablaze with glow of flowers and cresset fires,
Hears from a hundred joy-begetting lyres
  A storm of music roll from wall to wall,
  Yet feels no joy upon his spirit fall,
For all the while his wandering heart desires
One small sweet waif of sound those pealing quires
  May scorn—may drown, but never can recall.

Yea, seem I like that fabled king of old
Who gained his wish, and woke one morn—and lo !
With gold his bed and chamber were aglow,
  And when his glad arms did his child enfold,
  He clasped but to his heart a form of gold—
Gold roses in her breast, no more of snow,
Gold hair upon her gold and polished brow,
  Hard, bright the hands of which his hands took hold.

But from her golden trance he saw her wake,
Saw life and bloom return to all the flowers ;
Green grew again and fresh the wind-stirred bowers,
  And from its golden frost was freed the lake ;

But, though I drain my heart for *my* love's sake,
She will not come to make my waste of hours
Fruitful as earth beneath warm sun and showers,
  Nor quick with scent *my* scentless roses make.

Dear soul, to-night our wedding-night had been,
And death has come to you and fame to me;
The summer's breath makes music in the tree,
  Its kiss with over-love has charred the green,
  Through quivering boughs I catch night's starry-sheen,
A sense of unborn music seems to be
In air and moonlight falling tenderly,
  And yet I draw no sweetness from the scene.

O love, sweet love, my first, my only love,
How can I find the flowering meadows sweet
That no more feel the kisses of your feet!
  O silent heart that grief no more can move,
  O loved and loving lips, whereto mine clove
Till hope, long stanch, with thy heart's muffled beat
Furled his lorn flag and made his last retreat,
  And all was void below, and dark above.

Pale form, they should have clothed thee like a bride,
Have twined a bridal chaplet round thy head,
And decked thy cold grave as a marriage-bed;
   For, though the envious darkness do thee hide,
   I still shall find thee, sweet, and by thy side
Lie peaceful down while hands and lips shall wed,
And winds, attuned to lays of love we said,
   Float o'er the stillness where we twain abide.

   But now the gulf between us, love, is deep;
I labour yet a little in the fight,
And bear the outrage of the joyous light,
   I toil by day, and in the night I sleep,
   And then my heart gets ease, for I can weep;
But you in starless, songless depths of night,
With dreamless slumber shed upon your sight,
   Rest where none need to sow, or care to reap.

A GARDEN REVERIE.

I HEAR the sweeping fitful breeze
  This early night in June :
I hear the rustling of the trees
  That had no voice at noon :
Clouds brood, and rain will soon come down
To gladden all the panting town
With the cool melody that beats
Upon the busy dusty streets.

But in this space of narrow ground
  We call a garden here—
Because less loudly falls the sound
  Of traffic on the ear,

Because its faded grass-plot shows
One hawthorn tree, which each May blows,
Whereon the birds in early spring
At sun-dawn and at sun-down sing—

I muse alone.   A rose-tree twines
　　About the brown brick wall,　·
Which strives, when Summer glory shines,
　　To gladden at its festival ;
Yet lets, upon the path beneath,
Such pale leaves drop as I would wreathe
Around a portrait that to me
Is all my soul's divinity.

A face in nowise proud or grand,
　　But strange, and sad and fair ;
A maiden twining round her hand
　　A tress of golden hair,
While in her deep pathetic eyes
The light of coming trouble lies,
As on some silent sea and warm
The shadow of a coming storm.

From those still lips shall no more flow
  The tones that, in excess
Of tremulous love, touched more on woe
  Than quiet happiness,
When my arms strained her in a grasp
That sought her very soul to clasp,
When my hand pressed that hand most fair
That holds but now a tress of hair.

How look, this breezy summer night,
  The places that we knew
When all the hills were flushed with light
  And July seas were blue?
Does the wind eddy through our wood
As through this garden solitude?
Do the same trees their branches toss
The undulating wind across?

What feet tread paths that now no more
Our feet together tread?
How in the twilight looks the shore?
  Is still the sea outspread

Beneath the sky, a silent plain
Of silver lights that wax and wane?
What ships go sailing by the strand
Of that fair consecrated land?

How hard it is to realize
   That I no more shall hear
The music of thy low replies,
   As those deep eyes and clear
Once looked in my faint eyes until
I felt the burning colour fill
My face, because my spirit caught
In that long gaze thine inmost thought.

Alas! what voice shall now reply?
   Not thine, arrested gale,
That 'neath the dark and pregnant sky
   Subsidest to a wail.
On dusty city, silent plain,
And on thy village grave the rain
Comes down, while I to-night shall jest—
And hide a secret in my breast.

H

'MY LOVE IS DEAD.'

'Tis Spring, the fresh green glints in the brook,
The primrose laughs from its shady nook,
Winter away like a ghost has fled ;—
Let it be Spring, then—my love is dead !

The Summer is come with burning light,
The swallow wheels and dips in his flight,
The Spring away like a ghost has fled ;—.
Let it be Summer—my love is dead !

Autumn is come, with its gold-tressed trees,
Far through the wood sighs the dirge-like breeze,
Summer away like a ghost has fled ;— .
Let it be Autumn—my love is dead !

The Winter is come, with white, wan cheek,
The bare boughs toss and the wild winds shriek,
Autumn away like a ghost has fled ;—
Let it be Winter—my love is dead !

A VISION.

Lying between two sleeps, I did behold
  A vision strange, and terrible, and sad,
    Which seemed to me the key
    That opened all my wards of destiny.
Now listen, all who will, while I unfold
  The vision that I had.

Beside my bed I saw a man's form stand ;
  His brows were wasted as by wasting fire,
    Madness was in his gaze,
    Pain, with fierce lips, fed on his haggard face,
A gleaming serpent twined about his hand,
  Pale victim ot desire !

A strange and vivid wreath entwined his head—
  The myrtle green, the poppy, and the rose ;

Across his bare white feet
Did snakes again for fiery sandals meet ;
With blood the parched and pallid lips were red
That o'er his pangs did close.

Upon his limbs a fiery garment shone ;
At length, with lips unlocked, I heard him cry,—
'Oh, pain of great delight,
Be the sky fair with day or black with night,
'Tis all one thing to me, by sin led on
To where no tortures die !'

Dead, lying at his feet, I then did see
The figure of a boy still pure and fair ;
And by his side one knelt
Whose loveliness through every sense did melt,
As through the soul melts some wild melody :
Her supple limbs were bare.

Sea-blossoms quivered in her dazzling breast,
Roses and poppies round her brows did twine,
About her body burned
Splendour of crimson fire ; to me she turned,
Unto my sight the goddess stood confest,
Daughter of blood and brine !

Great Aphrodite gazed upon me there:
  Then I looked down upon the boy, and lo,
    His throat with blood was red;
    And now her fingers clutched the white throat dead.
I know not if he uttered any prayer,
  Or when she dealt the blow.

And then I saw, with wonder and great fear,
  The man's face, in a cold and death-set likeness,
    Upon the boy's face sweet;
    His eyes, his hair, his very hands and feet;
Their souls seemed far apart as sphere from sphere,
  Or blood from snow's cold whiteness.

And as I gazed a space with straining eyes,
  I saw the vision fading through the gloom;
    And, as it fainter grew,
    I heard, the thick and growing darkness through,
Fierce laughter, weary wails, then short, sad sighs—
  Then silence like the tomb.

FOREBODINGS.

Lo, I heard the sound of a sea
   That broke on a desolate shore ;
Then I said, ' O love, come back to me :
   Return to me, love, as before.'
And the sea cried aloud to the strand,
   ' She shall never come back again !'
And the wind blew it on to the land,
   And wearily wailed, ' It is vain !'
And over the waves that were high,
The moon came out soft in the sky ;
And her light was more sad than the sigh
   Of a saint for a spirit in pain.

I said to the waves, as they broke
   In splendour of foam at my feet,

'It is now all too late to revoke
   The past that was golden and sweet;
The moonlight, as tender as sleep,
   Lying long on your luminous ways
Would make souls less sad than mine weep
   For the dear and for-ever gone days.'
'Thy lot is more sad,' said the sea,
'Than thou knowest; and what is to be
We but vaguely foreshadow to thee;
   I in waves, as the moon in her rays.'

The sound of the wind as it blew
   Was more sad than moonlight or wave;
I said to the wind, 'Is it true?'
   The wind said, 'I am scooping a grave
Deep under the cold sea for one
   To your eyes fair, and dear to your heart
As the first burst of April sun
   Is to earth when the dark days depart.'
'Thy words tell of sorrow,' I said,
'If my love and my lady be dead,
The waves shall go over my head,
   And I of the deep will be part.'

The billows rose high with the gale,
  Clouds blotted the moon from my eyes,
The breakers broke foaming and pale,
  The tempest shrieked on through the skies.
I said to myself, 'I have heard
  The word of the wind and the sea.'
My heart was stung sharply, and stirred
  With hunger to know what should be,
I waited, and wondered, and paced
On the shore, by the desolate waste
Of the waters that, bitter and chaste,
  Spoke in tumult their message to me.'

.   .   .   .   .

.   .   .   .   .   .

Out at sea, far away from all shore,
  With tempest and death on each side,
All round her the clash and the roar
  Of the winds and the pitiless tide,
A vessel went down, and the place
  Where she vanished was hidden from sight ;

But, out of all faces, one face—
   A girl's face—flashed pale on the night ;
She looked out, as if looking for land,
She stretched through the tempest her hand,
As feeling her way to the strand
   Where a dead man lay rigid and white.

DEAD LOVE.

I SEE that you are weary with the dance ;
  Inside the air is faint with scent and light,
But here, where many-coloured lanterns glance
  Through trees whose branches quiver in the night—
Here let us stand alone a little space,
As in the days departed, face to face.

Your hair is not less golden than of old,
  Your eyes are not less sweetly fierce to snare
The souls of men, and still your curled lips hold
  The magic of a smile which was more fair
Years back to me than fairer things could be ;
And now its charm with flameless eyes I see.

Oh, how your face thrilled through me five years' since ;
The touch of this small hand I hold in mine

Would make my blood like fire, while lips would wince
   To feel your kiss; and as a shaken vine
That bows its straining branches to the wind,
So then to me you yearned with love made blind.

Then our lips clove, as if they ne'er would part,
   Then hands were linked with hands, and eyes met eyes;
Thus quickly never beats again my heart
   As in the days of that lost paradise,
For now as tunes played out, as poems said,
The music ceases, the closed book is read.

Then all the ways of life with bliss grew bright,
   As when in spring the long-delaying sun
Breaks through the sky and floods the land with light,
   And all the heaven's glory is begun,
Though yet before October ends, the skies
Look sad and strange as life-resigning eyes.

So shone our love which, ere late autumn time,
   Lay pale and dying with no breath for speech;
And now a withered rose, an empty rhyme,
   Is all that love so strong has left to each.

So tame love's fire, I gaze and snatch no kiss:
Alas! poor love, that it should come to this.

Let's sit beneath this lantern-fruited tree,
 That dances in the wind with jewelled light,
Let our souls backward look till they can see
 Some little glory of a gone delight:
Can you remember something of that time?
Or have you quite forgotten the old rhyme

I made that day of days when I and you
 Stood by the sea whose stormy shallows roared
On wastes of shell-strewn sand? The sky was blue
 As down the hot sun on the wet sand poured,
Up steamed the sea-scent warm, and sharp, and sweet,
We laughed to see the billows thundering meet.

None, save us twain, upon the shore was seen,
 The gull cried loud his short hard stormy cry,
The blown foam crested all the deep sea's green,
 The summer sun burnt hot, the wind was high,
Up hissing dashed the bright spray in our eyes
When a great wave broke with a great surprise.

But see how I have wandered from the verse
    Which I remember, though I see you doubt;
Laugh not, songs counted better I've deemed worse;
    A little love-sick song and all about
Your face and voice where still the old charm lies,
Sweet waifs of laughter and soft tender sighs.

It was a sad and happy time, you say,
    Yet sweet as is an ever-changing tune;
Ah me, the close of that still July day
    When with the sun's excess earth seemed to swoon,
And we together wandered on the shore,
Half feeling we should wander there no more.

All round the sea-wet shining nets were spread,
    Gold shone the cliffs and all the sea was bright
As through its glowing depths the sun had shed
    His soul in one great ecstasy of light,
Which fading, mutely we awhile did stand;
Then left for ever that enchanted strand.

Your goal was Paris: there one eve we went,
    Your mother with us.   How she loved to see

Our love !   That night the moon from heaven leant,
  As leans some maiden from a balcony
Down looking to the lawn with eager eyes,
To see a loved form through the stillness rise.

Recall the jingling horse-bells, the whip's crack,
  The still, lit villages where all was peace,
The hedges in the moonlight strange and black,
  The voiceless cornfields and the fleeting trees,
The long hill, wild and steep, which dashing down
We saw the tree-girt, white-walled, shining town.

Rattling into its narrow streets we plunged,
  And left the dim still country far behind;
The coach-wheels strained and thundered, whirled and lunged;
  At first the great light almost made us blind.
Ah, then, what laughs we laughed, what songs we sung,
While hands unseen, oft meeting, closed and clung.

As hot as ever Eastern desert was
  Grew Paris 'neath the blaze of August heat,
The public gardens, sad with withered grass,
  Seemed but to say—' Time was when we were sweet,

Before the south wind left us and the west;
Oh, once more in some grey cloud's shade to rest!'

But life hates joy; the war-cloud burst at length,
· And men of England girt themselves for strife,
Amongst them I : it tried my manhood's strength
    To kiss you the last time, perchance in life.
That night of thunder I remember yet
And how we parted can I not forget.

The earth with imminent tempest seemed oppressed,
    The torpid air shook shuddering to the sound
Of thunder booming slowly from the west :
    Long lurid light the vaporous greyness crowned,
And all things, with one stillness, ominously
Waited for that which was about to be.

The o'er-wrought heaven heaved and gasped in flame;
    Below black clouds hemmed in the fading light;
Incensed, the thunder cried aloud God's name,
    As one who warns the world ere he shall smite;
When suddenly up sprang a gusty breeze
And spread a panic through the swaying trees.

Then fiercer lightnings clove the sky in twain,
   Loud fell the thunder crashing through the sky;
A pause: then like redemption fell the rain,
   And hissed against the cracking earth and dry,.
Dark all around, save where the lightning's glow
Lit up the empty tree-fringed court below.

Oh, the last kiss, the long last lingering look,
   The touch and thrill of hands that intertwined!
But when at length the storm the sky forsook,
   I heard your voice rise mixing with the wind.
You say my voice was broken; so it was,
But did not yours, I think, in grief surpass.

Ah, think of how we looked, and what we said;
   Laugh as I laugh; your laugh is sweet to hear,
Love was our sovereign then rose-garlanded,
   He gave us pain, and bliss, and shame, and fear,
Now he is dead; yet know we not how slain,
But this we know—he shall not live again.

Out in the past, there let him lie and rot,
   He had his time of birth and time of death;

Give him one thought now, then remember not
  If ever his pale lips were warm with breath.
Oh, I am glad to-night, yea, gay enough
To dance a measure on the grave of love.

Nay, now at our past follies we can smile;
  I wept hot tears who had not wept till then,
No second love shall thus our hearts beguile:
  It happens to most women and most men
To know one love, which as a sudden fire
Burns and consumes their hearts with great desire.

Then all earth's fairness in one fair face lies,
  Then all earth's music in one sweet voice is,
Then 'neath the long rapt gaze of hungering eyes
  Love leaps to find its vent in one long kiss;
While cold and sad seems every other fate,
But we can smile now, only saying—wait!

You wedded joys that spring from wealth alone,
  I courted fame—a bright and barren bride,
Whom from Death's arms I snatched to make my own,
  When roared the red strife like a stormy tide.

I

Oh, very strange to-night this meeting is,
So much to feel, and yet one feeling miss :

That comes not back. Speak on, still, sweet, your voice,
   Years back it hurt me with delicious pain;
Let us shake hands across our buried joys.
   The waltz strikes up : you catch the well-known strain ?
When last we heard it 'twas that year in France,
Let us go in; your hand for the next dance.

GARDEN SECRETS.

THE DISPUTE.

The Grass.— I felt upon me, as she passed, her feet.

The Beech.—'Neath my green shade she sheltered in the heat.

A Rose.—She plucked me as she passed, and in her breast
Wore me, and I was to her beauty press'd.

The Wind.—And now ye lie neglected, withering fast,
And the grass withers too, and when hath pass'd
These golden summer days, O beech, no more
She'll sit beneath thy shade; but I endure
To kiss her when I will, so more than ye
Am I made blest in my felicity.

WHAT THE ROSE SAW.

The Rose.—Oh, Lily sweet, I saw a pleasant sight.

The Lily.—Where saw you it, and when?

The Rose.—Here; when the night
Lay calmly over all and covered us,
And no wind blew, however tremulous,
I heard afar the light fall of her feet
And murmur of her raiment soft and sweet.
The Lily.—What said she to thee when she came anear?
The Rose.—No word, but o'er me bent till I could hear
The beating of her heart, and feel her blood
Swell to a blossom that which was a bud.
Alas, I have no words to tell the bliss
When on my trembling petals fell her kiss;
Sweeter than soft rain falling after heat,
Or dew at dawn was that kiss soft and sweet.
Then fell another shadow on the ground,
And for a little space there was no sound;
I knew who stood beside her, saw his face
Shining and happy in that happy place,
I knew not what they said; but this I know
They kissed and passed : where think you did they go?

THE ROSE AND THE WIND.

DAWN.

The Rose.—When think you comes the wind,
The wind that kisses me and is so kind?
Lo! how the lily sleeps; her sleep is light;
Would I were like the lily pale and white;
Will the wind come?
The Beech.—Perchance for thee too soon.
The Rose.—If not, how could I live until the noon?
What, think you, Beech-tree, makes the wind delay?
Why comes he not at breaking of the day?
The Beech.—Hush, child, and, like the lily, go to sleep.
The Rose.—You know I cannot.
The Beech.—Nay, then, do not weep.
The Beech.—(*After a pause*): Thy lover comes, be happy
      now, O Rose,
And softly through my bending branches goes.
Soon he shall come, and you shall feel his kiss.
The Rose.—Already my flushed heart grows faint with bliss;
Love, I have longed for thee through all the night.
The Wind.—And I to kiss thy petals warm and bright.

The Rose.—Laugh round me, love, and kiss me; it is well.
Nay, have no fear, the lily will not tell.

Morning.

'Twas dawn when first you came, and now the sun
Shines brightly and the dews of dawn are done.
'Tis well you take me so in your embrace;
But lay me back again into my place,
For I am worn, perhaps with bliss extreme.
The Wind.—Nay, you must wake, love, from this childish
    dream.
The Rose.—'Tis thou, love, seemest changed; thy laugh is loud,
And 'neath thy stormy kiss my head is bowed.
O love, O Wind, a space wilt thou not spare?
The Wind. —Not while thy petals are so soft and fair.
The Rose.—My buds are blind with leaves, they cannot see,
O love, O Wind, wilt thou not pity me?

Evening.

The Beech.—O Wind, a word with you before you pass,
What didst thou to the Rose that on the grass
Broken she lies and pale, who loved thee so?
The Wind.—Roses must live and love, and winds must blow.

THE GARDEN'S LOSS.

A Lily.—He will not speak to us again,
No more the sudden summer rain
Will fall from off his trembling leaves,
Even the scentless tulip grieves,
Ah me, the loud noise of that night,
And that fierce blaze of blinding light
That slew him in the midst of bliss,
Stretch out, O Rose, and let us kiss.
The Rose.—He was a friend to all indeed ;
Even the wild unlovely weed
Loved him and clove unto his root :
When next winds blow he shall be mute.
The Lily.—He was the noblest of all trees.
A Tulip.—Your sorrow cannot bring you ease.
The Lily.—Still we must mourn so great a one.
The Rose.—I would the summer time were done.
The birds we loved sang in his boughs,
And in his branches made their house ;
All graciously he bowed and swayed,
And, when of winds we were afraid,

How tenderly his boughs he moved,
A loving tree and well beloved.
An Elm.—He was a noble tree and vast,
His branches revelled in the blast,
I always took him for our king ;
Yet better that he was so slain
In midst of his loved wind and rain,
Than some sharp axe should lay him low.
The Rose.—Better ; but now I only know
He shall not speak again to me,
Nor, lily, shall he speak to thee.

A CHRISTMAS VIGIL.

ROUND the vast city draws the twilight gray ;
> 1 know men say,
This evening is the eve of Christmas Day,
But what has Christmas time to do with me,
Who live a shameful life out shamelessly ?
A creature now that doth not even yearn
> From sin to turn ;
Too blind perchance it may be to discern
God's mighty mercy, and the boundless love
That all paid, praying preachers .tell us of.

Here he lies dead, with whom my shame began,
> This is the man !
Through whom my life to such dishonour ran.
He was the snare in which my soul was caught ;
Oh, the sweet ways wherein for love he wrought.

Yet God, not *he*, my wrath of soul shall bear,

        God set the snare !

God made him lustful, and God made me fair.

O God! were not his kisses more to me

Than Christians' hopes of immortality?

O lovely, wasted fingers, lithe and long,

        So kind and strong ;

O lips! wherein all laughter was a song,

All song as laughter.   O the cold, calm face,

The speechless marble mouth, that had such ways

Of singing, that for very joy of it,

        My heart would beat

Almost as loud as when our lips would meet,

And all love's passion, hotter for its shame,

Set panting mouths and thirsting eyes on flame.

Thus, would I part his hair back from the brow ;

        But look you now,

What thing is left for me, save this, to bow

Myself unto him, as in days gone by,

To stretch myself beside him, and to die ;

To crush my burning, aching lips on his,

      In one long kiss;

To know how cold and strange a thing death is?

His lips are cold, but my lips are so hot,

That all death's fearful coldness chills them not.

Fast falls the night, and down the iron street,

      Loud ring the feet

Of happy people, who pass on to meet

Fair sights of home; I hear the roll and roar

Of traffic, like a sea upon a shore.

One dying candle's pallid light is shed

      Upon the bed

Whereon is laid my beautiful, cold dead,—

Mine, altogether mine, for two brief days!

Are not these hands his hands; this face his face?

And now I can recall the time gone by,

      The pure fresh sky

Of spring, 'neath which we first met, he and I,

The smell of rainy fields in early spring,

The song of thrushes, and the glimmering

Of rain-drenched leaves by sudden sun made bright,
The tender light
Of peaceful evening, and the saintly night.
Sweet still the scent of roses; only this,
They had a perfume then which now I miss.

Yea, too, I can recall the night wherein
Did first begin
The joy of that intoxicating sin.
Late was the day in April, gray and still,
Too faint to gladden, and too mild to chill;
Hot lay upon my lips the last night's kiss,
The first of his:
I wandered blindly between shame and bliss;
And, yearning, hung all day about the lane,
Where, in the evening, he should come again.

Now, when the time of the sun's setting came,
The sky caught flame;
For all the sun, which as an empty name
Had been that day, then rent the leaden veil
And flashed out sharp, 'twixt watery clouds, and pale,

Then, suddenly, a stormy wind upsprang,
>> That shrieked and sang;
Around the reeling tree-tops, loud it rang,
And all was dappled blue, and faint, fresh gold,
Lovely, and virgin; wild, and sweet, and cold.

Then through the wind I heard his voice ring out,
>> And half in doubt,
Trembling and glad, I turned, and looked about,
And saw him standing in my downward way,
Full in the splendour of the dying day.
Silent I stood a space, and then at last
>> Strong arms were cast
About me, and his burning spirit passed
Into my spirit, till the twain as one
Shone out together under passion's sun.

I felt that joy unnameable was near;
>> A great sweet fear
Fell all around me, and no thing was clear
To me save this,—that in his arms I lay,
And felt his kisses burn my soul away.

I heard the wild wind singing in my hair,
And saw the fair
Green branches tossing in the stormy air ;
And, through the failing light, I heard a voice
That cried, ' O soul, at least this night rejoice !'

Ah me ! the shameless, limitless delight
Of that spring night !
The magic ways wherein, 'twixt dusk and light,
I wandered, dazed and faint with joy's excess—
Ah, God ! what human creature shall express
That night's dear joy, the long thirst quenched at last,
All shame outcast,
The haven entered, and the tempest passed ?
O shameful, sacred night, whereby alone
I bear with life till life's last day be done !

But when the feverish night had passed away,
And faint, and grey,
On wet, chill April fields calm broke the day,
I rose, and in an altered world had part ;
Love, marred by shame, lay bitter at my heart.

Through all my daily rounds that day I went,
Till day was spent ;
And with the night once more came sweet content,
And joy that shut out every thought of shame,
And made all infamy an empty name.

Then quickly came the waste, gold, summer days,
The blinding blaze
Of burning sunlight, and the sultry ways
Of breathless nights, wherein the moon seemed strange,
And with the scent of roses came the change ;
Yea, when, as naked blades sharp-edged and bright,
'Neath blasting light,
Sharp flashed the streams ; when every coming night,
Solemn with moonlight, or with stars thrilled through,
Or quite unlit but passionately blue,

Were sweet as rest—'mid song, and scent, and flame,
To me there came
The sense of loss, and bitterness of shame.
Surely between his kisses he had said,
' O love ! before the summer time has fled,

I will return, and thou with me shalt come
                                   To a fair home.'
My kisses answered, for my voice was dumb.
Ah, God ! those terrible June days, wherein
No rapture came to hush the voice of sin.

O sickening perfume of those summer days !
                                   O tree-girt ways
Wherein we wandered ! O the happy place
Where first I burst on love, and love on me !
O sleepless nights when tears fell bitterly !
So died the Summer ; and the Autumn sweet,
                                   With languid feet ;
And recollections of the by-gone heat
Came down to us ; but still he came no more,
And then I knew my destiny was sure.

I know not how, at length, when hope was gone,
                                   And shame had grown
Too sharp a thing to be endured alone,
I left the peaceful country far behind,
And to the mighty city came to find

Some opiate for pain, and found it, too.
                    Fresh passions grew
Within me : and a little while I knew
The bitter joys that set the blood on flame :
So grief slays joy, and wretchedness slays shame.

But still, through every feverish night and day,
                    The old love lay
Hot at my heart, though he had gone his way,
As I had mine : sometimes of him I heard,
And how the world was by his spirit stirred.
Then came the news, how he lay dying here !
                    I shed no tear,
I only felt the time at length was near,
When meeting I should see his face again,
And feel, through all, I had not lived in vain,

And now it is two nights ago, since first
                    With eyes athirst
To see his face, resolved to know the worst,
I came in here, and stood beside his bed :
No look he gave me, and no word he said ;

K

But I said, bowing down, and speaking low—
                        ' Two years ago,
You slew my honour, and I come here now
To tell you, whether yet you die or live,
Lost as I am, I love you, and forgive.'

He turned, and then I knew that he would speak;
                        Against my cheek
Hot beat the blood, I stood there dazed and weak;
He said—' O face and voice that I remember,
'Twas July then, and now it is December;
Poor dove! that all God's hawks for prey have got.
                        Ah me! how hot
This fever burns, and she remembers not
The ways of love wherein last June we trod!
They work their will, this woman and her God.'

Thus, as towards ending of his speech he drew,
                        I only knew
Some other bitter mem'ry had come through
His thoughts of me, and set his soul adrift;
Then, as he backward fell, I saw him lift

Bright hollow eyes unto the wall, whereon
                    A picture shone—
A picture now that from the wall has gone ;
A portrait of a woman strange as fair,
With calm grey eyes, and fitful gold of hair.

The pale calm face, immovable and sad,
                    Such beauty had,
As well might make by love a strong man mad.
The long sweet hands upon her breast were laid,
The full throat just a little back was swayed,
Its firm white beauty better to expose ;
                    The mouth kept close
The spirit's secrets of all joys and woes ;
So calm and still he lay, I thought he slept,
Till, bending nearer down, I knew he wept.

                    .

And then he said, as one who speaks in dreams,
                    ' O face that gleams
Upon me when in sleep my spirit seems
To walk with thine, O long-loved love, O sweet,
O vanished eyes, O unreturning feet !

'O heart that all the tempest of my love
                              Could no way move !
O death, is not the end now sharp enough —
To love her, and to lose her, and to die,
While she knows not how life is going by?

'Could she know, all I think she would arise,
                              And let her eyes,
Wherein the very calm of heaven lies,
Fall on my face ; yea, too, I do believe
So sweet her sweet soul is that she would grieve
A little space, in silence sitting here,
                              To see draw near
Death's sea o'er which no light and land appear ;
Yea, too, with words and touches she might make
The death-ward path smile as a flowering brake.'

Then all his love came on him, and he cried,—
                              'O death ! divide
My soul from thought of hers ; O darkness ! hide
The passionless cold face and speechless mouth
By mine unkissed that waste my soul with drought !

'O love, and must I die unkissed by thee?
                                    What man shall be
The chosen one to come 'twixt thee and me?'
Then forth into the air he stretched his hand,
As one who, drowning, strives to reach the land.

Upon his brow a trembling hand I laid,
                                    And tearless said,—
'Lie down and rest.' Then, as the rain is shed
When awful thunder-storms break up the heat,
My kisses on his lips and eyelids beat,
My fingers met and closed within his hair,
                                    He was so fair;
And, like the unhoped granting of a prayer,
Such prayers as dying men for life must pray,
At length upon my hand his kisses lay.

Then by him, bowed with all my love, I fell,
                                    - And cried, "'Tis well,
Live yet, and in thy presence let me dwell.'
He smiled, and said, 'O tender hands and kind,
O lovely worshipped hands that now I find

So sweet, so sweet ! O love, that bringest bliss,
                              What joy is this
To gain at last the heaven of thy kiss?'
And then he turned himself, gave thanks and sighed,
Nor spake again; and in the dawn he died.

My lips sealed up his eyes, my hands were spread
                              Beneath his head.
I stretched the lovely limbs upon the bed,
Folded the wasted hands upon the breast;
As there he lay in calm and frozen rest,
The drawn and rigid lips looked cold and stern,
                              That seemed to spurn
All joys and griefs; no soul was left to yearn
Within the hollow, dreamless, lampless eyes,
Whose death-look said the dead soul shall not rise.

I know not whether I did wrong or right,
                              But in the night
I came into his room, and raised the light
Unto the pictured face upon the wall
That looked on his, and was not moved at all;

I took it down, the face indeed was fair;

                        But, standing there,

I spurned it with my foot as God spurns prayer,

And lacking strength, not will, to spoil the face,

I cast it forth where none might know its grace.

And yet I think sometimes if he could know,

                        Loving her so,

As men, O God, can love and bear with woe,

He might be angry for the face downcast,

And for it come to hate me at the last;

But now the heavy tread upon the stair

                        Of men who bear

Some strange thing up: they come, they will not spare.

O God! they come, and now the door goes back;

They smell of death, the thing they bear is black.

SHAKE HANDS AND GO.

COME now, behold, how small a thing is love;
  How long ago is it since, side by side,
  We stood together, in that summer-tide,
  And heard the June sea, blue, and deep, and wide,
Murmuring as one that in her dreams doth move
  To thoughts of love's first kiss and beauty's pride?

How long is it? But one brief year ago;
  One autumn, and one winter, and one spring;
  Now, as last year, the birds awake and sing,
  Once more unto the hills the hill-flowers cling;
How is it with you? What heart you have, I know,
  Changes with every comer and fresh thing.

And yet, I think, you loved me for a space;
  At all events you loved my love of you:

Whether to me or that, your love was due
I know not ; while it lived perchance 'twas true ;
But you forget each season and each face,
And love the new as long as it is new.

Scan o'er that time, as at the close of day
One thinks what he has done or left undone ;
Know you those days when noontide heats of sun
Smote full upon us, and we strove to shun
Their flaming force, and took the sheltered way
Of shading trees with green leaves softly spun ?

There in an island of dim green and shade
We stretched, while round, like a great silent sea,
Lay the blue, blinding, burning day ; but we
Knew nothing save our own life's melody,
And there, until the day was done, delayed ;
Then homeward wended o'er the dewy lea.

Know you those moonlit nights spent on the sand—
The golden sand beside the lucid deep—

Where soft waves rippled as they sang in sleep;
How there we sowed what I alone shall reap?
Nay, feign not thus to draw away your hand,
  Nor droop your lids; I know you cannot weep.

O pliant crimson lips and bright cold eyes,
  Lips that my lips have pressed, and fingers sweet
  That lay about my neck, or soft, would meet
  Around my eyes to screen them from the heat,
Where are your words, where is our paradise?
  Your love was warm as summer—and as fleet.

And yet, behold, with some how strong is love;
  How helpless is the dupe that boasts a heart!
  I know you now—and yet regret to part:
  Fairer than ever, in the marriage mart
You'll fetch your price; time's dealings that are rough
  With nature, leave untouched the works of art.

Well, kiss once more as in the gone-by time,
  Let your hair mix with mine, take hands again;

Your kiss is sweet—and do you only feign?
There, look once more on jutting cliff and main;
And now go hence, while I in some sad rhyme
Weave our love's tale—its brief joy, lasting pain.

Go, go thy way; return not to the gates
Of the fair past, forsake the dear dead days;
I know thou wilt. I to some distant place
May wander and forget your voice and face:
No anger, say 'Good-bye!' I know one waits:
He paid his price and for his purchase stays.

TO A CHILD.

I KISS you, dear, and very sweet is this,
To feel you are not tainted by my kiss;
   Cling with your warm soft arms about me so,
   Give me one small sweet kiss and murmur low,
In speech as sweet as broken music is.

How long shall God my Lily darling give
Untainted by the shrieking world to live,
   I cannot tell; but this my wish shall be,
   Longer at least than God has given me,
But still be glad; as yet, you need not grieve.

There, see, I put the hair back from your face,
And if my lips in kissing should displace
   Your sunny hair, you will but laugh, my child,
   A babbling silver laugh and undefiled.
God keep it so, through the all-ruling days.

But, I, who in the darkness sit alone,
With heart that, once rebellious, now has grown
   Too weak to strive with foes that smite unseen,
   Will only ask you once your head to lean
Upon a heart where grief has made his throne.

I will not tell you of the things I know,
I cannot bar the path that you must go ;
   God's bitter lesson must be learnt by all,
   But living, I will listen to your call,
And stretch to you a hand that you may know.

You feel the wind against you as you run,
And love its strength, and revel in the sun ;
   So once did I, and but for this last blow,
   Of which none know save me, so might I now ;
But now for me the light of life is done.

These little hands that lose themselves in mine,
May some day haply in a man's hair twine
   While 'neath their touch his heart shall palpitate,
   Then shall this soul with triumph be elate
And mix sharp poison in a maddening wine.

But see you keep your lips from tasting sweet,
For it begets within us such a heat,
   As cooling waters never can allay.
   We see, through mists of blood and tears, the day,
Until we sicken for the nightfall's feet.

There, there, you're weary, and I let you go,
But this kiss, softer than a flake of snow,
   I will remember when alone I stand.
   I wonder will you ever understand
The reason why I loved and kissed you so.

A SONG OF THE STORM.

Across the barren moor
We hear the breakers roar,
See them shine upon the shore ;
   Hear, loud, the sea-gulls cry :
The wind blows loud and shrill,
The sea heaves hill on hill,
Moonlight and tempest fill
   The pure and stormy sky.

'Neath clashing winds of night
The sea revels in its might,
And clear the pale, blown light
   Of driven billows gleams.
O bright, tempestuous sea !
From whose gaping foam-mouths flee
Ships hunted to the lea,
   As souls by evil dreams.

If only I might share
That strife of sea, and air,
Nobly to do and dare
    Would make my heart rise high,
As a martial soul's desire,
That, at sound of trump and lyre,
Breaks into flower of fire,
    While the wind of sound goes by.

O women with rent hair,
The wind beats back your prayer,
Which may not reach to where
    The loved ones strive for life.
Can all your tears appease
The anger of the seas,
Or make a night of peace,
    With sea and wind at strife!

Sea-shrieks come loud and long,
Through the thunder and the song
Of breakers white and strong,
    Exploding on the land.

Against the cliffs the wind
Strikes madly, being blind,
What shall the day-break find
   Upon the barren strand ?

O white and windy deep,
How many millions sleep
'Neath thy valley and thy steep;
   O bright careering sea !
O white, warm, bubbling spray,
Blown hissing all one way,—
O loud, resounding bay !
   O lorn and stricken lea !

Thou, God, in whose clear sight
The day is as the night,
Man's weakness as his might,
   The tempest works Thy will,
Obeys, is stayed by Thee :
Say to the wind and sea,
Peace ! and a calm let be,
   And all the tumult still.

THE LAST REVEL.

So now our one month's love is done.
    Good-bye, my love ! good-bye !
Before to-morrow's burning sun
    Flames golden in the sky,
We shall be far apart, my sweet,
No more, no more to meet.

How well I know this chamber, dear,
    A blaze of mirrors tall ;
The lattice too, wherethrough we hear
    The sighing water fall
Upon the steps that from the sea
Lead up, my love, to thee.

Lo ! how the softened lamp-light rests
   Upon your gleaming hair ;
Upon your splendid foam-white breasts,
   Bright shoulders curved and bare.
Let 's fill once more the goblet up,
And kiss across the cup.

How hushed the great warm heavens are ;
   The sultry moonlight lies
Upon the sea, and one vast star
   Possesses all the skies.
Down the dim water streets we see
The boats glide dreamily.

Sing me again the song I heard
   You sing that first sweet night,
When, to my senses stained and blurred,
   O'er wastes of glaring light,
In all the glory of the song,
Your voice came clear and strong.

But first from instruments there stole
   Strange music, soft and low,

I felt through all my wearied soul
  The gentle music flow:
And in the tender harmonies
My heart lay faint with peace.

And when again you sing that song,
  And all men cry your name,
Some thought of me may lurk among
  The thoughts of gold and fame ;
You may perchance recall this night,
And all our past delight.

You say you will remember well ;
  The speech sounds sweet and smooth,
And though I know for gold you sell
  The kisses of your mouth,
Your eyes keen fires, your hair's bright hue,
Yet still it may be true.

And so you thought me cold at first,
  My calm eyes chilled your bliss ;
But when you saw my lips athirst
  To taste your longed-for kiss,

You found me better, did you not?
Girls like a man's blood hot.

But when the passion fades away,
   The chill comes back, you think;
'Strange was that Englishman,' you'll say;
   'He kissed, and he could drink,
And in the middle of a feast
Be solemn as a priest.'

And did it never strike you, love,
   That in his heart might be,
That which your kiss was not enough
   To banish utterly;
A thought he could not quite shut out,
Yet could not speak about?

How if grief snared him in his land,
   And tracked him o'er the sea?
A grief from whose relentless hand
   He never might get free;
A grief that slept not in the night,
But murdered all delight.

A grief, which, when you sang your best,
   Outsang you with its voice,
Chanting in pain, and long unrest,
   Its dirge for buried joys ;
A sadder song than ever man
Sang since the world began.

I do not say it is so, mind,
   Only, if so it be,
You might perchance some reason find
   To wonder less at me ;
But vain to speak to you of this,
Who sell, not give, love's kiss.

I take you in my arms again ;
   O shoulders bright and smooth,
Soft throat whereon my kisses rain,
   Keen eyes and glowing mouth ;
Once more I feel a strong blood yearn
   Within my veins, and burn.

What is the gift you give to me,
   And what the gift I give ?

I hold the right your face to see
  As long as I shall live,
And you this bracelet like a snake,
To wear a day — and break.

THE GARDEN.

'TIS easy of one thing divine
  A smooth and pleasant song to sing,
Perchance some small strength might be mine
  In worthy verse to praise the Spring.
But where all different beauties meet,
  As in the subject of this rhyme,
My song would almost make retreat
  Much wanting strength, more wanting time.

Each look, each grace, each smile, each tone,
  Long years of sacred labour ask.
And then by failure should be shown
  The greatness of the hopeless task ;
For failure here more than success
  Is the best tribute man can pay ;
Words fail the spirit to express
  And baffled homage owns dismay.

Yet look a little up, my song,
   Compose yourself to some sweet tune,
Think of the shining days and long,
   The splendour of the summer noon,
The warm still garden, flushed and fair,
   Full of the summer's tender noise,
While flowers with scent beguile the air,
   For perfume is the rose's voice.

Seems she not such a garden meet?
   Gracious and happy giving bliss,
A garden where all beauties meet
   Of every sound and scent that is,
With roses and with lilies white
   That garden is most fair to see ;
With flying music and sweet light
   More fair than earthly gardens be.

Yet is this but one lovely phase ;
   For, as that garden is in spring
When all the wind-clad laughing days
   Come dancing down the land, and bring
The warm sweet rainy gusty smell
   Of violets blowing fresh and free,

While birds with high clear voices swell
    The west winds' waving minstrelsy;

So in her lighter moods she seems,
    Yet none can deem, no man can say
Which of her many moods he deems
    Would be most sweet his soul to slay.
Alas, it matters not at all,
    Hers is the noble victory;
Our souls must bow, our hearts must fall,
    In most divine captivity.

The gods determined at her birth
    To make one soul which should o'er-reign
All other souls upon the earth,
    Therefore all singing is in vain.
The gods rose up, '"Tis good,' they said,
    'Though all you poets say 'tis wrong,
That we so fair a thing have made
    Which art defies and baffles song.'

·

A MEDLEY.

A LILY are you? such you seem,
　A lily brimmed with dew and scent;
With languid, listless leaves that gleam,
　By heat made sweetly indolent,
　While all the sky with love is hot,
　Such love as Earth remembers not
When June is but a lovely dream.

You seem in soul a panther bright,
　With velvet paws, but made to slay;
A lily laughing in the light,
　A panther seeking after prey:
　A panther fair, with noiseless tread,
　A lily, with bowed stem, and head,
Lapped in the loveliness of night.

So very fair, the smallest thing
  On which you look at once looks fair ;
And but to hear you play and sing,
  Would make with envy Orpheus swear.
  Forgive me, if I leave a space,
  The lily and the panther phase,
Your touch, and voice remembering.

To be of all men's hearts the Queen
  Is surely, lady, good enough ;
Your looks are sweet, your words are keen,
  To first exalt, then humble love.
  'Tis better far to worship thee
  Than Venus, old world deity,
Whose loveliness is praised unseen.

And men years hence shall know you as
  One lily-formed and panther-souled,
The gods themselves did quite surpass
  Your spirit and your form to mould.
  They made you as a poet makes
  His best rhyme when his hand so shakes
It scarce can hold the pen or glass.

More clear than notes of music be
　　Your voice, in no two words the same ;
A sudden burst of melody
　　To glorify with sound a name ?
　　With ear and eye assailed at once,
　　Against such fatal needle-guns
The man who would be safe must flee.

A poem with a double sense,
　　A joy, a grief, a tiger-lily,
With images I now dispense ;
　　My flower I leave in the wild nook hilly,
　　In the forest the panther fleet,
　　My song is kneeling at your feet,
Give it one smile for recompense.

A curious medley is this verse
　　Of lilies, poets, panthers, guns,
I may sing better or sing worse,
　　But no more thus my swift verse runs ;
　　For soon I write a song most fit
　　To be in ladies' albums writ
And read by all the universe.

BEFORE BATTLE.

HERE in this place, where none can see,
   Lean out your throat, and let us kiss ;
Who knows, to-morrow I may be,
   As far from any joy like this,
As is my own sea-beaten strand,
            From this fair land.

She put the hair back from her face,
   And kissed him on his eager mouth ;
Her kiss was warm, and long her gaze,
   He felt the passion of his youth
Burn fierce through every thrilling vein,
            Till it was pain.

He filled for her a cup of wine,
  The sparkling wine as red as blood,
She quickly drank, and for a sign
  He kissed its edge, as saints the rood,
Before Death plucks their souls away,
            Too faint to pray.

He said, 'O love, the wine is sweet,
  But, sweet, thy kiss is sweeter still!'
She flushed, with sudden joy and heat,
  She said, 'O love, then take thy fill
Of both these things, for both thine are,
            Before the war.'

Another cup of wine he quaffed,
  Then in his arms her form he pressed,
He murmured low; she sighed and laughed,
  And they clung fiercely breast to breast:
While all her hair fell round his face,
            Her love to grace.

She thrilled with passion, till her lips
　Could nothing do, but kiss and cleave,
Their souls were like sea-driven ships;
　He felt her swelling bosom heave;
His lips her lips with kisses flaked,
　　　　　·　Till both lips ached.

His face above her fair, flushed face,
　Now seemed a thing to wonder on;
Her soul was ravished by his gaze,
　Her warm, wet eye-lids shook and shone,
Till, leaning back, for pure delight,
　　　　　She laughed outright.

He wrung her long sweet fingers out,
　He strained the passion at her mouth,
Her hair was all his face about,
　O life to life! O youth to youth!
O sea of joy, whose foam is fire!
　　　　　O great desire!

But, suddenly, a sharp shrill sound
    Cut like a sword their dear delight;
Once more his arms about her wound,
    They felt their pulses beat and smite.
At last he said, in accents low,
              ' The foe ! the foe !'

Then quickly from her arms he sprang ;
    For all the night-black winding street
With clash of deadly weapons rang,
    And sudden storm of passing feet ;
She heard the thunder of the drum.
              Her lips grew dumb.

' O one night's love ! Good-bye !' he said,
    And kissed her on the lips, and passed.
She heard his quick, departing tread,
    She saw the torches glare at last,
She saw the street grow light as day,
             And swooned away

An hour afterwards, or more,
 With stormy music, loud and long,
With light behind, and light before,
 The men marched down, an arméd throng :
And as they passed, he saw her light
    Still burning bright.

She from her chamber-window leant,
 Deep down into the street to gaze ;
Her head upon her hands was bent :
 He looked, but could not see her face ;
But still he thought, through sound and flame,
    She cried his name.

She watched the torches fade away,
 She listened till the street grew still,
Then back upon her bed she lay,
 Of her own thoughts to drink her fill ;
And afterwards, when others wept,
    She only slept.

Next night she revelled in the dance,
   She quaffed her wine, she sang her song ;
While he, with soldier's eyes askance,
   And heart with lust of slaying strong,
Leaped laughing into battle's hell,
               And struck and fell !

UPON THE SHORE.

ALL, love, is as it was this time last year,
  When we together stood as now we stand,
  By the same sea, on the same curving strand ;
And, as last year we heard, as now we hear,
The rippling of the water cool and clear !

The old grief still goes with me near and far,
  Like the sweet burden of a mournful air
  Full of the sadness of unanswered prayer,
Not sad with discords strange that strike and jar,
But sad as early autumn twilights are.

And you ? You know I do not blame you, sweet ;
  My lot was sore and had but little ease,
  And his was smooth and soft, a path of peace ;
Ah, well it was, love, that the path was smooth
For your soft beauty and your untried youth.

Let us recall the past a little space—
  That night of summer storm when on the shore,
  We heard athwart the sea the thunder roar,
And sound of rising wind, and saw the blaze
Of lightning all about the sea-girt place.

That night you leaned your head upon my breast,
  And now upon another breast you lean ;
  O days gone by, O days that might have been !
To love is good no doubt, but you love best,
A calm safe life with wealth, and ease, and rest.

Gifts he will bring no doubt, each mood to please,
  And make life soft and pleasant for your feet,
  But will he give you love like mine, O sweet,
From which my heart can never know release
Till death and darkness bring me perfect peace ?

Nay, let us once take hands before we part,
  You bore, half prized, my love a little while,
  'Twas something that long summer to beguile !
There, see I kiss the hand that cast the dart,
You gave me grief and I gave you my heart !

WAITING.

WHEN shall I see that land where I would tread
That shrine where I would fain bow knee and head?
In autumn—ere the autumn pass, I said;
In winter—ere the winter time is sped,
In spring—ere yet spring's fair sweet feet are fled,
In summer—ere the summer time is shed—
And now I say, perchance when I am dead.

IN PRAISE OF.

WHAT thing is there on earth to which I can
                    My love compare?
So far she is beyond all praise of man,
                    That speech is bare,
                    To say how fair,
She is beyond comparison.

Her nature seems like some warm summer sea,
                    That bears alone
The utmost glory, and the majesty
                    Of all the sun,
                    Till day be done;
Then takes the stars for company.

As children who for cooling waters crave,
                    On some hot day;

And in the ebb of the retreating wave,
Are glad to play,
And feel the spray,
Their gleaming, panting bodies lave.

So in the shallows of her nature, we
Are glad to move.
I know not if on earth a man there be
Found strong enough,
The depths thereof
To reach, in calm security.

Yea, all the music of a summer deep,
Her tones possess;
Such melody as comes when light winds sleep
And souls confess
Joy's keen excess,
In tears that are most sweet to weep.

O deep kind sea! O passionate strong sea!
Thy deep tides flow
'Twixt God's vast life, and our mortality.
Yet who shall know,
Where thy waves go,
For few know where the strand may be.

IN GRIEF.

With thee so vanished our life's light has flown,
  A sudden night has fallen on the day—
  A cheerless, moonless night with no white way
Of stars that lead to lands of men unknown.
    A night wherein the winds of grief are loud,
    A night made black with sorrow as a cloud,
    A night that wraps its darkness as a shroud
Around a world now sad, and cold, and gray.

God fashioned thee and gave thy spirit birth
  To ease a little our sore load of pain ;
  More sweet to us thy love was than the rain
Is after long, hot days to burnt-up earth.
    Thou wert a refuge in a stormy deep,
    From thee there flowed a peace like conscious sleep.
    I will not sow sweet things who may not reap,
    I will not strive who nothing here may gain.

As is to one within his dungeon's gloom
  A sudden burst of music and of light,
  Cleaving the darkness, trancing ear and sight,
Making resplendent what is still his tomb;
    So living to my prisoned soul thou wert;
    Now all once more is dark about my heart,
    No light, nor any sound its depth shall part,
  And there shall be no daybreak to this night.

Now all is done; no more is left to do:
  A space we stood together on life's shore
  Waving weak hands to those who went before;
Thou knowest now if heavenly skies are blue,
    Thou knowest if the after world is sweet,
    Dost thou tread light or darkness 'neath thy feet?
    When with weak hands upon the gate we beat
  Will it be opened, or closed evermore?

And shall we meet with lips that yearn to kiss,
  Meet soul to soul as face to face on earth?
  And shall there be an end of death and dearth,
Yea, shall there be a harvest time of bliss,

And shall we stand together side by side
Never again to sorrow or divide ?
And shall at length our hearts be satisfied
Full of the wonder of the second birth ?

Shall this life past be as a dream outdreamed,
  The ghastly fancy of a fevered brain ?
  Shall we at all remember the old pain
So great it past all human bearing seemed ?
    If angels tell us of that mournful time,
    Will it then sound but as an empty rhyme
    Made by a boy in some forgotten clime ?
  Ah, shall we say we have not lived in vain ?

Shall we stand up before the face of God,
  Stand up and sing a loud, glad song of praise,
  And bless him for the sorrow of our days,
And kiss with pure cold lips the burning rod
    Wherewith he hath so stricken us that we
    Might come at length within his home to be,
    Laid in the light of his divinity,
  First blinded by the glory of his face ?

Oh, strange and unseen land whereto we come,
  Are thy shores shores of day or shores of night?
  As near we draw shall we indeed see light,
And shall we hear, through lessening wind and foam,
    The voice of her we love come from the land,
    And, looking shorewards, shall we see her stand
    Girt round with glory on a peaceful strand,
  Smiling to see our dark skiff heave in sight?

I cannot know; there is no man who knows;
  We are and we are not, and that is all
  The knowledge which to any may befall:
We know not life's beginning nor life's close,
    'Twixt dawn and twilight shine the sunny hours
    Wherein some hands plucked thorns and some hands
      flowers,
    'Twixt light and shade are shed the sudden showers;
  Yet night shall cover earth as with a pall.

Sadder than all thou art, O song of mine,
  Because thou callest vainly on her name,
  Because thou fain wouldst rise and sudden flame
Before God's face and her face most divine,

And tell her of the bitter grief we feel,
And pray her by some sweet sign to reveal
The land which God and darkness so conceal—
Say where our sorrows lead and whence they came.

O saddest of sad songs by sad lips sung,
Fresh hopes may rise, fresh passions snakelike hiss,
Or fresh illusions find fresh rods to kiss;
But joy is fleet and memory is long.
And on the fair sweet reaches of the past,
Lovely and still, for evermore is cast
A sad and sacred light which shall outlast
The fierce and short-lived glare of summer bliss.

Alas, poor song, all singing is in vain,
What thing more sad is left for thee to say?
Oh, weary time of life and weary way,
Can dead souls rise or gone joys come again?
Now by the hand of sorrow are we led,
Though sweet things come, they come as joys born
    dead;
Let us arise, go hence, for all is said,
And we must bide the breaking of the day.

MISCELLANEOUS SONNETS.

BEREFT.

I WILL not mock thy memory most dear,
By striving to describe what soul was thine,
A soul which never more shall look on mine.
I cannot talk of any higher sphere,
Nor can I make the utter darkness clear ;
I know no God, I worship at no shrine,
I only bow before thy life divine !
I will not tell of voices that I hear,
I will not tell of secret bitter tears ;
I will not tell of desolated years,
Of sunless springs that come to ravaged lands,
Of altered seas that break on altered strands :
My heart has only room this thing to know,
Thou once wast with me, and thou art not now.

TO ——.

O YEAR ! while others crowned with pleasure sit
To watch thee slowly, darkly pass away,
To thee, so dying, I at least will say,
O bitter year, that with remorseless feet
Didst tread down all whereby my life grew sweet,
Didst thou not turn the golden into grey
And snatch the very sunlight from my day?
Yet, now that thou art dying, it is meet
That ere thou goest quite, for one sweet thing,
One, only one, I give thee thanks, O year!
The knowledge of a friend, now found so dear
That she a little can bring back the spring
To fields that seem forgotten of the light—
A star to bless my moon-deserted night.

DESOLATE.

I STRAIN my worn-out sight across the sea,
I hear the wan waves sobbing on the strand,
My eyes grow weary of the sea and land,
Of the wide deep and the forsaken lea :
Ah ! love, return ! ah ! love, come back to me !—
As well these ebbing waves I might command,
To turn and kiss the moist deserted sand !
The joy that was, is not, and cannot be.
The salt shore, furrowed by the foam, smells sweet,
Oh ! blest for me, if it were now my lot,
To make this shore my rest, and hear all strife
Die out like yon tide's faint receding beat :
If he forgot so easily in life,
I may in death forget that he forgot.

FORSAKEN.

Would God that I were dead and no more known,
Forgotten underneath the deep cold main,
Freed from the thrill of joy and sting of pain;
There I should be with silence all alone,
To weep no more for any sweet day flown!
I should not see the shining summer wane,
Nor feel the blasting winter come again,
Nor hear the autumn winds grow strong and moan;
But time, like sea-mist screening the far deep,
Should make each hated and loved object dim,
And I should gaze on both with hazy sight;
God granting this, I should no longer weep,
But, wearied, rest beneath the clear green light,
And surely lose in sleep all thoughts of him!

FIRST AND LAST KISS.

Thy lips are quiet, and thine eyes are still,
Cold, colourless, and sad thy placid face,
Thy form has only now the statue's grace ;
My words wake not thy voice, nor can they fill
Thine eyes with light.   Before fate's mighty will,
Our wills must bow; yet for a little space,
I sit with thee and death in this lone place ;
And hold thy hands that are so white and chill.
I always loved thee, which thou didst not know,
Though well he knew whose wedded love thou wert ;
Now thou art dead, I may raise up the fold
That hides thy face, and, by thee bending low,
For the first time and last before we part,
Kiss the curved lips—calm, beautiful, and cold !

NOT LIVED IN VAIN.

HAVE I not worshipped thee in tender lays,
And told in barren rhymes my love for thee ;
And now I wish that I no more might see,
Or ne'er had seen your fair, alluring face ;
Or, as a tune felt your lithe body's grace
Melt through my heart that leap'd up eagerly
With joy of hope ; now hope no more may be ;
For hope lies dead, amid the dear, dead days.
Still, if the bitterness of unshed tears,
And burden of a spirit sorely tried,
Did e'er with joy of maiden's victory fill
Thy woman's heart, then surely these sad years
Have been well lived, nor, sweet, would I have died,
Till thy heart had of mine, its perfect will.

CHANGELESS.

THE Spring, a maiden beautiful and pure,
Wearies of earth, and leaves the happy lea;
The stormy winds grow weary of the sea;
The sailor lad grows weary of the shore,
Tunes that charmed once fail always to allure.
Weary we grow of grief and too much glee,
We weary captive, and we weary free:
Suns set, moons rise, the stars do not endure.
Let this be as it is; but this I know,
Though life, grown weary, parts at length from me,
Though joy remembered turns to deepest woe,
Yea, though as one our lives may never be;
Through life, in death, where none may reap or sow,
My love, O sweet, shall weary not of thee.

ACROSS SEAS.

TO BJORNSTERN BJORNSON, AUTHOR OF 'ARNE.'

I.

I, TOILING here through many weary days,
Turn from the extreme bitterness of pain,
As turns a journeying sailor from the main,
In middle sea to rest, a little space,
On some soft island where his hands may raise,
'Twixt land and sea a rough and rocky fane,
Whereat his God to worship, ere again
Unto the stormy waves he sets his face.
So, ere I pass, a little yet I turn,
And raise, apart from all, to thee a shrine,
And render homage in these trembling lays,
Which, could they higher rise, and clearer burn,
Might reach a little from my soul to thine,
Not past man's worship, but beyond man's praise.

.

II.

FOR, looking downward from thy spirit's height,
Things that we cannot see to thee are clear;
Music by us unheard thou yet canst hear;
And, as men read the wonders of the night,
So dost thou read with clear unfailing sight
These hearts of ours, and, from thy higher sphere,
Canst see in Spring the Autumn dawning near,
Canst in the darkness see the unborn light,
Canst see how love, ere yet men know its name,
Fed with cool dews of dreams, begins to bud,
Ere yet it break into a blossom bright,
Whose warm and trembling petals shine as flame;
A flower that fades not when the summer wood
Lies chilled and leafless in the winter's blight.

III.

Sweeter than half heard music is to one,
Who waits upon a summer's night, and sees
The warm, white moonlight slanting through the trees,
And smiles to think the glad time is begun ;
Sadder than, when the summer time is done,
The autumn twilight when the fitful breeze
Sighs for the year's lost prime and sunny ease ;
So is to me the web thy soul has spun
Of dream-flowers plucked from pale, dim fields of sleep,
Warm with no sun, wet with no rain of ours :
Surely the web was woven well of these,
And in the streams we know not did God steep
The opening blossoms, and the full-grown flowers —
Hopes born of griefs, and joys of memories.

IV.

So end these rhymes that lack the magic wing,
Which could alone bear up my thoughts to Thee,
Oh ! soul unseen, though not unknown of me ;
Yet, as in winter thinking of the spring
Doth seem more near the distant May to bring —
As one who worships prone on bended knee,
Then nearest seems unto his God to be ;
So—with like hope, a little while I sing,
And bow in soul, and worship in this rhyme;
And from my land to-night, I look afar,
Until I almost deem that I can see
The snowy mountains of that northern clime,
In midst whereof, as flames a winter star,
Thy spirit shines in its divinity.

SPEECHLESS.

Upon the Marriage of two Deaf and Dumb Persons.

THEIR lips upon each other's lips are laid ;
Strong moans of joy, wild laughter, and short cries
Seem uttered in the passion of their eyes.
He sees her body fair and fallen head,
And she the face whereon her soul is fed ;
And by the way her white breasts sink and rise,
He knows she must be shaken by sweet sighs ;
But all delight of sound for them is dead.
They dance a strange, weird measure, who know not
The tune to which their dancing feet are led ;
Their breath in kissing is made doubly hot
With flame of pent-up speech ; strange light is shed
About their spirits, as they mix and meet
In passion-lighted silence, 'tranced and sweet.

TO SLEEP.

O TENDER Sleep! Queen over ev'ry queen,
Our mother, since from thy deep womb we spring,
And unto thee return, and to thee bring
Our weary limbs and wearier hearts, and lean
Upon thy breast; thou who hast saddening seen
Our woe on earth, and blunted life's sharp sting,
And when we were in trouble did so sing,
That we forgot what was and what had been ;
Open thy gentle arms and take me in ;
Hide me! oh, hide me in thy mother's breast,
Between thy bosom sweet, and long, soft hair;
Yea, let me from thee drink the milk of rest :
Lay all my virtue level with my sin,
So that I have no thought of days that were.

A MOOD.

BEHOLD !   How fair it is to see in Spring,
The frozen river once more thaw and run
Under fresh wind, and warm, soft, flickering sun,
Is it not good to dance and laugh and sing,
To feel somewhile the lips of pleasure sting?
Lo ! now the fairness of a love well won ;
But then things pass, and some day Spring is done,
And, since we see there are no joys that cling,
Would it not be far wiser to have none?
Time's tide is dark and bitter with our tears,
Why should we swell it with the greater pain
Of fair gone things, a few, glad, golden years ?
Of one sad colour let our days be spun,
So we may live, nor weep to see life wane.

LOVE'S ILLUSIONS.

A WOMAN strange, and beautiful to see,
With limbs of light and hair of the sun's gold !
Her fair hand did a mighty goblet hold ;
The bubbling wine thereof shone dazzlingly,
So that I said, ' Now, even give to me
Some of this wine that sparkles bright and cold.'
She gaily laughed, and said, ' Thou art too bold,'
And went her way, and heeded not my plea.
But I said, ' She will come again,' and bore
The present bitter for a coming sweet ;
And lo ! she came, but passed me as before,
And came yet after this, but held no more
The goblet filled with wine of life and heat,
That stains now, and makes wet, God's hands and feet.

SLEEPLAND GLORIFIED.

ALL nights my lady comes to me to rest,
Contentedly in quiet vales of sleep;
And sometimes, those sweet eyes of hers will weep,
And barren tears make wet each white, round breast.
Once only were her lips to my lips prest;
Then in my veins I felt love's passion leap,
And all the blood-red waves of pleasure sweep
Across my heart that might not be repress'd,
But found its vent in kisses thick and sweet,
That fell upon her mouth and quivering eyes,·
While all her gracious body shook with sighs;
And we were wedded then, as was most meet.
No light shone round, no music breathed, save this:
Love's moan of joy, and murmur of his kiss.

SLEEPLAND FORSAKEN.

O LOVE! O sweet! where art thou gone, my love?
I tread the songless ways of sleep alone;
In sleepland's shadowy caves I make my moan.
O sleep's pale, waveless, voiceless seas whereof
She seemed a part—where is the syren gone?
O whispering forests, tell me of the dove!
O paths with lilies and with roses sown,
Where is my flower, the fairest of the grove?
O sweet, unanswering voice and feet so flown,
In vain along the silent shore I rove
Where shadows of the moon-lit rocks lie prone,
By tideless seas that never winds may move!
Alas, my God, their depths are deep enough
To hide that face, and they shall keep their own.

JUSTIFICATION.

I CHARGE you lay on this dead man no blame :
Had not God so his mighty spirit cursed,
Not set his hand against him from,the first,
We now had had as great and pure a name   .
As ever flashed through all the world like flame.
Had not his soul been wasted by this thirst,
Until his o'erwrought heart was nigh to burst,
He had not drank so deeply of this shame.
The hands of God are strong to make or mar,
And if He gathers clouds about one star,
Who says that star is least among the rest?
I swear by these blank eyes and tortured breast,
Though I should take upon me God's worst ban,
'Tis God that I abjure, and not this man.

LOVE'S WARFARE.

'AND are these cold, light words your last?' he said,
And rose, his face made pale with outraged love.
She answered gaily, 'Are they not enough?'
And lightly laughed until his spirit bled,
While snake-like on his grief her beauty fed.
He looked upon her face once more for proof,
Then through and through his lips the sharp teeth drove,
Till with the bitter dew of blood made red.
At length he said, 'And so 'twas but a jest,
A well-conceived, well-executed plan;
Yet now may God forgive you, if God can!'
And, passing, left her calm and self-possessed.
She watched him cross the lawn with eyes bent low,
Where she had kissed his face one hour ago.

LOVE'S TRUCE.

She speaks no word, but, stretching out her hand,
Touches him softly where asleep he lies;
And he, too feeble now to feel surprise,
Awakes and faintly smiles: they understand.
But now her fragrant breath his brow has fanned,
He raises to her face large, hungry eyes,
While like entrancing music fall her sighs
Upon his heart long exiled from joy's land.
For she, repenting of a deed ill done,
Bows, kissing tenderly his white, chilled face,
And in the dim gold twilight of her hair
His eyes grow blind, he feels her last embrace;
Then on her breast his head sinks unaware,
And life goes nightwards with the setting sun.

COUNSEL.

IT takes us such long time to understand
That God is God, and man can be but man ;
We live and labour for a little span,
We wait, and watch, and fertilise our land,
And all for what ? that war's all-wasting brand
May spread its dearth according to God's plan ;
And still we vainly strive beneath the ban,
And think against this God to set our hand.
Oh, all my brothers, rest a space from strife,
Let each one with no murmur live his life.
Will ye make glad our tyrant's eyes and ears,
By sound of sighs and sight of bitter tears ?
Not so ; but rather spite the God on high,
By showing Him how men can live and die.

IN BONDAGE.

OH! I have waited long for thee, my sweet,
In these cold dungeons far from light or day,
And wondered if your eyes were blue or gray,
And how your face would look, my face to meet;
And yet his vengeance cannot be complete,
Who holds me here as pris'ner in his sway,
And, as a panther lurks about his prey,
He lurks about us now with noiseless feet.
Yet kiss me once upon the lips and bow
The solemn beauty of your face to mine,
Laugh as you laughed of old; but why turn pale,
And why does such sweet rising music fail?
Ah! he hath fill'd the cup to overflow,
And I must drink your tears for my last wine.

TO A TUNE.

O WILD, sweet tune, of which my soul is fain,
Through the loud sound of sea and tempest heard,
Like the low moan of a wind-driven bird,—
O sad, sweet tune ! O passionate, wild strain !
Full of past joy, dead hope, and present pain,
Once more I catch thee, and my heart is stirr'd,
Stung sharply by that one great, simple word, ·
Gone as a dream that shall not come again.
Once more I see my lady's warm, flushed face,
See her deep amorous eyes, and swept back hair,
Yea, hear the tender sobbing of her breath.
O tune ! made sad with all sweet things that were,
O tune ! keep back, or quite restore those days,
That, past, crown life or break our wills for death.

TO A DAY.

SHALL I sing of the earth or of the sea?
Of bright-wing'd Mirth, that stays its hour, and flies,
And then doth perish in sad alien skies;
Shall I praise these, O Day, and not praise thee
That giv'st me rare, sweet gifts—yea, was to me
A's sudden fire, and perfume in mine eyes,
That made my roused, stung heart to swell and rise,
Filling it with the joy of joys to be?
The year returns, but thee I see no more—
'Gone as a man's first dream of goodness goes;
But, where less joys are as forgotten things,
When I draw near to the pale, shadow-shore,
Be with me then, to fight against my foes;
Kiss me, and guard me! hide me with thy wings.

STRONGER THAN SLEEP.

WEARY, my limbs upon my couch I laid,
And dreamt; and in my dream I seemed to see
My lady, who was soon my bride to be,
Silently standing, gazing on my bed,
A crown of bright red roses on her head.
I said, ' O love ! this hour is sweet to me ;
Stretch out your throat and let us kiss.'   Then she
Bowed down her body and brows garlanded.
' Stretch out your hand and feel,' her deep eyes said :
I touched, and through soft raiment felt her form
Panting and glowing with the want of love.
Then all the waves of pleasure, deep and warm,
Burst through my veins.   My eyes love's hot tears bled,
And I awoke, too weak to speak or move.

SHAMELESS LOVE.

THY food my body, and my blood thy wine,
My soul too thine, to tread beneath thy feet,
While thus my hair is gold and my breast sweet,
Most rapturous is this shameful life of mine.
But time must come, between my life and thine,
When I must leave the heaven of this heat,
And through the cold, grey twilight go to meet
The night wherein no stars nor moon may shine.
A rose, then withered by fierce passion's sun,
Left soiled and trampled in the public way,
A broken wine-cup emptied of delight;
Yet would I not, to triumph o'er that day,
Give up one wild, sweet moment of this night,
That finds once more love's tune of joy begun.

· STRICKEN!

O LOVE, behold thy feet are shod with flame!
Thy body clothed with torture as a dress;
Too weak thy stricken lips are to express
Thy mighty grief, or call upon the name
Of Him who gives the sorrow and the shame.
Thy lips have tasted the salt bitterness
Of tears like blood, wrung out of thy distress.
Thy soul must reap a barren, bitter fame.
Fair lands beneath thee, and fair skies above,
Thy heart falls blind outside of that fair land
Whereto it may not come; all words are vain—
It is the unattainable we love:
But rest a little, and a friendly hand
Shall give thee peace, and ease from all thy pain.

ABOVE LOVE. ·

COME now, I will be frank with you, and say ,
I have for you a strange and bitter love :
Most strong it is, but no love's strong enough
From higher aims to make me turn away ;
Some short sharp pain, some idled night or day
Is all the hurt that I shall have thereof.
I will not wed you, and I must remove
Your spirit from my path, as best I may.
Your face would come between my work and me,
Your love would quite unnerve me for the strife ;
Kiss me, forget me wholly, as I know
I shall forget you in the whirl of life.
Nay, do not look ; I swear I will not see ;
Take off your lips lest I should crush you so.

THE FIRST KISS.

SHE sat where he had left her all alone,
With head bent back, and eyes through love on flame,
And neck half flushed with most delicious shame,
With hair disordered, and with loosened zone;
She sat, and to herself made tender moan,
As yet again in thought her lover came,
And caught her by her hands and called her name,
And sealed her body as her soul his own.
The June moon-stricken twilight, warm, and fair,
Closed round her where she sat 'neath voiceless trees,
Full of the wonder of triumphant prayer,
And sense of unimagined ecstasies
Which must be hers, she knows, yet knows not why;
But feels thereof his kiss the prophecy.

BOUNDED LOVE.

ALL ways of common love pall on me now!
No kiss the madness of my thirst allays,
Through all my wild warm dreams deep burns thy face,
And, when I wake, I hear thy love-laugh low,
As all the amorous blood is set a glow.
Oh, for some hymn of unconjectured praise,
Some unimagined splendour of new lays,
Wherein love bounded, might at length o'erflow.
Oh, for an ocean of new deed and speech,
Where, no more cramped, our spirits might toss free,
As ships that revel in full wind and sea,
That living, yet beyond life, we might reach
To find some fresh lights, deep and strong enough
To bear the mighty burden of our love.

CONJECTURE.

I THINK, love, as I hold your hand in mine,
If starless, cheerless, everlasting night
Should settle suddenly upon my sight,
And I should no more see your eyes divine,
Or golden lights that in your tresses shine,
Or face now made my measureless delight,
Or sweet curved throat, warm, beautiful, and white,
Or soft, lithe arms that round about me twine,
How should I bear to sit with you as now,
And if you looked upon me not to know ;
To hear men praise your throat, mouth, eyes, and hair,
Yet feel to me you were no longer fair ?
To miss the blush that colours all your kiss,—
Slay me outright, O God ! but spare me this.

TO M. C., ON HER VISIT TO LONDON IN WINTER.

SHUT are the summer's golden gates, I said,
Gone are the life and light, and gone the bloom ;
Now turn we sadly to the winter's gloom,
Pale, silent lands beneath our feet to tread,
Cold wastes of grey sky stretching overhead.
But, while afar we saw the winter loom,
Fate came between us and the coming doom ;
Summer he claimed, but gave us thee instead.
Then fairer glowed the earth than in June days,
Sweet sounds, more sweet than sounds of summer be,
Hearing your voice, we heard.   The darkest place,
If you but through it passed, grew light as day,
And if again in spring we meet not thee,
Then shall December triumph over May.

CAPTURED THOUGHT.

A THOUGHT came to my spirit as I lay
Between two sleeps, and, through the silent night
It looked at me with sudden eyes and bright ;
But, when I strove to touch it, fled away,
And bade me dream ; but at the break of day
I, waking, saw, through grey, increasing light,
My last night's thought ; but as, with greater might,
I strove to grasp it, only crying ' Stay !'
It spread its wings for flight.   Then, as a snare
I set my song and snared the lovely thing,
And said, ' O flying thought, thou art too fair
For me to leave thee free and wandering !
Yet fret not for thy liberty, but where
Sad souls can hear thee be content to sing.'

SUPPLANTED LOVES.

WHEN first the music of your voice I heard,
Methought love's mystic promptings did arise,
And gathered strength beneath your gentle eyes;
My being to its depths was strangely stirred,
For you, I think, by look and tone averred
Your heart was mine: yet, as a meek star dies
When slow, resistless daylight fills the skies,
So softly waned that love when one deferred,
Transcendent passion lit my life—its sun !
·Upon your nature rose a kindred light,
To quench my ray; and yet our half-born fate
Perchance no future can obliterate;
But, bliss fulfilled recalling bliss begun,
We four shall walk together in God's sight.

LONDON : STRANGEWAYS AND WALDEN, PRINTERS, Castle St. Leicester Sq.

Now Ready.

A SERIES OF SIXTEEN ETCHINGS.

By JAMES WHISTLER, Esq.

Price to Subscribers only 12l. 12s. in a handsome portfolio.

N.B. One hundred Copies only have been printed, and nearly all are subscribed for.

Fifth Edition, crown 8vo. cloth, 8s.

THE LIFE AND DEATH OF JASON:

A Poem, in Seventeen Books.

By WILLIAM MORRIS.   .

" Morris's ' Jason ' is in the purest, simplest, most idiomatic English, full of freshness, full of life, vivid in landscape, vivid in human action—worth reading at the cost of many leisure hours, even to a busy man."—*Times*.

MR. SWINBURNE'S NEW POEMS.

SECOND EDITION.

Now Ready, in Ornamental Binding, designed for the Author, 10s. 6d.

SONGS BEFORE SUNRISE.

By ALGERNON CHARLES SWINBURNE.

" There is, we believe, more real poetic power shown in this volume than in any of the poet's earlier works."—*Saturday Review*.

FIFTH EDITION.

Crown 8vo. in an Ornamental Binding, designed by the Author, price 12s.

POEMS.   .

By DANTE GABRIEL ROSSETTI.

" Here is a volume of poetry upon which to congratulate the public and the author ; one of those volumes, coming so seldom and so welcome to the cultivated reader, that are found at the first glance to promise the delight of a new poetical experience.   There is no mistaking the savour of a book of strong and new poetry of a really high kind; no confounding it with the milder effluence that greets us from a hundred current books of poetry, in various degrees praiseworthy, or hopeful, or accomplished ; and we may say at once that it is the former and rarer savour that is assuredly in the present case to be discerned."—*Pall Mall Gazette*.

LONDON: ELLIS & GREEN, 33 KING ST., COVENT GARDEN.

MR. MORRIS'S GREAT POEM.

THE EARTHLY PARADISE:

A Poem, in Four Parts.

(SPRING, SUMMER, AUTUMN, AND WINTER.)

Now complete in 4 vols. crown 8vo. cloth, price 2l., or separately—

PARTS I. and II. (Spring and Summer), 16s.
PART III. (Autumn), 12s.
PART IV. (Winter), 12s.

These Volumes contain Twenty-five Tales in Verse, viz.:—

PARTS I. AND II.

THE WANDERERS.	THE LOVE OF ALCESTIS.
ATALANTA'S RACE.	THE LADY OF THE LAND.
THE MAN BORN TO BE KING.	THE SON OF CRŒSUS.
THE DOOM OF KING ACRISIUS.	THE WATCHING OF THE FALCON.
THE PROUD KING.	PYGMALION AND THE IMAGE.
CUPID AND PSYCHE.	OGIER THE DANE.
THE WRITING ON THE IMAGE.	

PART III.

THE DEATH OF PARIS.	THE MAN WHO NEVER LAUGHED
THE LAND EAST OF THE SUN	AGAIN.
AND WEST OF THE MOON.	THE STORY OF RHODOPE.
ACONTIUS AND CYDIPPE.	THE LOVERS OF GUDRUN.

PART IV.

THE GOLDEN APPLES.	THE RING GIVEN TO VENUS.
THE FOSTERING OF ASLAUG.	BELLEROPHON IN LYCIA.
BELLEROPHON AT ARGOS.	THE HILL OF VENUS.

"We must own that the minute attention Mr. Morris bestows on scenic details he also applies to the various phases of human emotion, and ofttimes he fills the eyes with sudden sorrowless tears of sympathy with some homely trouble aptly rendered, or elevates our thoughts with themes charming in their pure simplicity, and strong with deep pathos."—*Times.*

"A thorough purity of thought and language characterises Mr. Morris,....and 'The Earthly Paradise' is thereby adapted for conveying to our wives and daughters a refined, though not diluted, version of those wonderful creations of Greek fancy which the rougher sex alone is permitted to imbibe at first hand. Yet in achieving this purification, Mr. Morris has not imparted tameness into his versions. The impress of familiarity with classic fable is stamped on his pages, and echoes of the Greek are wafted to us from afar both delicately and imperceptibly.......Suffice it is to say, that we have enjoyed such a thorough treat in this, in every sense, rare volume, that we heartily commend it our readers." —*Saturday Review.*

LONDON: ELLIS & GREEN, 33 KING ST., COVENT GARDEN.

www.ingramcontent.com/pod-product-compliance
Lightning Source LLC
Chambersburg PA
CBHW030120030726
47498CB00007B/2479